THE GARDNER

How We Grow, Book 1

SONYA YOUNG

Edited by
CAROL WILLIAMS

Illustrated by
BOBBY BARNHILL

LAKEVIEW
PUBLICATIONS

CONTENTS

Prologue 1
1. The Unknown 5
2. The Mountains 7
3. SOMEWHERE-Home 9
4. Valo 13
5. BEFORE SOMEWHERE-Previous Home 17
6. BEFORE SOMEWHERE-First symbol 21
7. BEFORE SOMEWHERE-Shower 23
8. BEFORE SOMEWHERE - Changing 27
9. BEFORE SOMEWHERE - Meditation 31
10. SOMEWHERE-Home 35
11. Glimpse Into The Unknown 39
12. SOMEWHERE – The Meadow 41
13. SOMEWHERE – The forest 47
14. The Tree 51
15. Recover and Realize 59
16. Glimpse Into The Unknown 61
17. Seeds 63
18. Bees 69
19. First Hive 73
20. Funerals 77
21. Reya and Mehlin 83
22. Life Is the Answer 87
Reya's Notes 91
23. Glimpse Into The Unknown 97
24. The Mountains Sit Up 99
Epilogue 109

Glossary 111
Acknowledgments 113
Also by Sonya Young 115
About the Author 117

Printed in the United States of America

First Printing, 2021

ISBN: 978-0-578-25313-8

Book Cover Design: Bobby Barnhill
Editing: Carol Williams
Formatting: Craig A. Price
Publisher: LakeView Publications

For future generations to come. For my children I've yet to meet and for the grace that follows life after life.

GRATITUDE

I am grateful for the scientists: the silent warriors in the background who stand watch over our planet, awaiting the next spark of brilliance to fuel their creativity.

I am grateful for the apiculturists who are literally saving our lives with every breath they breathe into a new hive. I am eternally grateful for your tenderness toward these sacred creatures.

I am grateful for the farmers, closest to the earth, the voice of the soil, for your tireless dedication with every crop, never knowing the outcome until you harvest. You are the risk-takers and the dreamers and the nurturers to us all. Thank You.

Finally, to the explorers and the seekers. It is your fascination, curiosity, and willingness to go beyond yourself which guarantees our very existence. I am grateful for your courage and your fearlessness in the face of the Unknown.

I stepped on a weed today.
I stepped on a weed by choice today.
I was walking in the park like I normally do and chose the same
path that I normally take.
This morning didn't feel like any other morning. I love it there
in the park and I love watching my puppy run and jump and
play in the warm green grass.
Today I bounded toward a hill and looked down at my feet and
made a conscious choice to step on a bunch of weeds instead of
the grass.
This choice struck me right in the Moment my foot crushed
the crisp green leaves.
I could feel the leaves snap under my weight while the sound
vibrated through me, loud and clear, and I realized in that
Moment that I had judged the weed.
I decided the weed was less important than the warm plush
green grass. I decided that if given a choice I desired crushing
the weed instead of the grass.
In this Moment I recognized my judgement and found it
shocking to me.
Disturbing that I never noticed before the indiscriminate walk
I take daily.
Disturbing that in this Moment, given the choice, I chose
based on a belief, and, most disturbingly, that I took pleasure in
choosing what I believed was of more value.

I stepped on a weed today and recognized it.

PROLOGUE

T uuli and Meri look down on their son and thank the
moon and the stars for sending them such a vibrant
being. Meri holds him close to her chest as Tuuli beams, alive
with pride. They never thought this day would come. They
were told they couldn't have children. They were told to give up
and move on with their life; that is, until they visited Anushka
at the Apothecary.

She took one look at them without any hesitation and told
them they would be parents.

"In fact, you will be parents of a brilliant child whose life
will impact many others."

She smiled and handed them a cup of tea blended for the
sole purpose of experiencing joy.

Avaruus lies in his crib, looking out the skylight in the ceiling.
His dark blue eyes are almost as black as deep space with gold
around his iris; his face is captivating. He can see the night's sky
filled with stars and ambient light from the city. He stares until
he falls asleep. Avaruus dreams of space. While other children

cup their stuffed animals, dreaming of games and playgrounds, he dreams of galaxies and interconnections between them. At six months old, he is communicating from his heart to the Unknown and the Unknown is answering back with pictures of places no one has ever seen before.

By age seven he is communicating with giants, at least that is what he tells his mother. Meri is not too concerned; she knows children have make-believe friends.

"What are your giant friends' names?"

"Well, there is Yli and Lasna, Viime and Tulevaisuus, and there are others, but they haven't given me their names yet."

"Why not?"

"They are waiting."

"Waiting for what?"

"Waiting for the right Moment."

"Well, while you are waiting, go upstairs and make your bed then come back down for breakfast. You don't want to be late for school."

"Yes, Ma'am."

Meri and Tuuli had many conversations with Avaruus that were unusual. He would tell them that he felt space inside himself. When he closed his eyes, he could see rotating galaxies and stars light-years away.

"It's inside me, Mom." Meri would stroke her son's hair and tell him that he was amazing or brilliant and that he should keep imagining.

When Avaruus was sixteen, he told his parents that he felt himself changing from the inside out. He felt all of these sensations running through his body that he couldn't explain, but they excited him. He told Meri at night he'd hear a girl's voice calling out from the unknown.

"What is she saying?" Meri asks.

"Hello. Can you hear me? Is anybody there?"

"I've tried to talk back," Avaruus continued, "but she's never heard me."

Later, Meri looked at Tuuli and told him that he had to have "the talk" with their son. She felt that Avaruus was going through puberty and his hormones were kicking in.

Frustrated with them both, Avaruus would tell his parents that they didn't understand. It was the frustration which prompted Meri to encourage Avaruus to visit the Apothecary and meet the woman responsible for his birth.

Frustrated and out of sorts, he pushes open the Apothecary doors. With his first step inside, his hair begins to sparkle.

CHAPTER 1
THE UNKNOWN

The Unknown is rarely visible to humans although it occupies a dimension of their world. Their eyes are not designed nor were they ever meant to see or understand this place. There are no sounds, smells, tastes, nor colors visible to a human's five senses. As a result, a human would never survive here. Their minds could not handle the nothingness and would crack if they remained here. Mind you, the nothingness is what their bodies would interpret. This is not to say there is nothing here. There is plenty. Plants, flowers, trees, and nature know of its existence. They know there are vein-like structures that run throughout. Like a network of channels, the veins carry information, emotions, technology, discoveries. Describing the network might be like the network that exists on a tiny leaf. There are highways and byways for different things and the colors change depending on the needs. The leaf attracts what it needs from nature just like the veins communicate with the multidimensional.

A human would also not sense that this place is protected by a circle of swords. The swords are made from elements and metals not on any periodic table nor listed in any chemical compounds' manual, but they are swords, nonetheless. They are vibrating together, making a hum that cannot be heard by the human ear. You don't need to understand this place or even see it to believe it exists. How could you? The swords vibrate, veins pulsate, and the air that is not oxygen mixes with them causing manifestation. It is said that a few rare humans have caught glimpses of this place, but the veil that gently protects this dimension from theirs will not unveil itself to just any being. Recorded visions of the Unknown are perhaps just misinterpretations in the end. The sacred secrets of the universe lie just beyond the veil. A veil woven by the fibers of manifestation and existence and held together by space. The veil and the Unknown are not affected by time; however, it is only through time that humans feel the evolution of this space.

CHAPTER 2
THE MOUNTAINS

I f you asked them, they can't recall when. One day they were walking the earth and decided to stop in this exact spot to lie down, their massive bodies creating a series of mountain ridges. They do not realize they appear as mountains; they are giants after all. Their heads push through the clouds. Although resting on the Earth, they are not earthly. They feel connected to something vast and wide. **Viime** (Past), **Lasna** (Present), and **Tulevaisuus** (Future) are the three most prominent ridges in the mass of mountains in this area. They occupy space in the air and the land. Their actions are powerful but normally unobservable by people.

Viime watches her intently. She is a stranger to this land. A newly arrived stranger and they are unsure of her. She hasn't lived on the land for long, but the mountains feel her presence. People come and go from this place all the time and they barely notice. Viime stirs inside, creating a current that is creeping toward Lasna and Tulevaisuus. Like striking a match to light a candle, a spark ignites a blue flame inside the three ridges. There is a disruption in the ridges, and they want to know why.

Viime feels that it is the girl who lives in the home just beyond the forest and the meadow causing it. The mountains are alive and awake, watching, feeling, sensing. They are intrigued and look across the land for answers.

CHAPTER 3
SOMEWHERE-HOME

The air is crisp with a slight touch of moisture in it. A shiver starts at her feet and radiates until it reaches her shoulders where her chiseled blackish-brown hair rests. She hurries to grab a throw from a hook by her bed. Dark-colored symbols arise from beneath her skin, marking her left and right shoulders. The blanket gently passes over the symbols and light emits from beneath the throw as they sense the blanket's comfort for her. Her mysterious hazel eyes shimmer, especially the golden rings that encircle the iris. A ring of heritage and lineage that she now knows connects her to things beyond her understanding.

She looks delicate but strong. Her body is fortified by the wisdom that flows through her like the blood through the rest of her body. Her hands are marked with symbols, too, but these are much smaller. They fade in and out, almost like switches being turned on with or without her knowledge. She is self-conscious about them. Mainly because she doesn't know how she got them or why. When she is in public, she covers them, concerned that others might see them. Easier this way, she thinks; easier than explaining something she doesn't understand. When she is alone out here in her sanctuary, however, she spends time trying to get to know them.

Reya is excited by the feelings of what is possible ever since she moved here. She glances out the window to the mountains for the first time today. These mountains are her strength and her friends. She talks to them and says prayers to them in the morning. She loved them the Moment she saw them in her mind's eye. It was seeing these mountains that launched her on a journey to find them. The mountains, although a fleeting glimpse imprinted upon her so vividly, she wouldn't rest until she stood in their shadow. It took her over a year to find the mountains. When she did, she purchased a home with an unfettered view of the three most prominent ridges.

Her home is spacious but cozy. It looks humble from the outside but filled with the riches of time and the awareness of things that make a home feel precious and safe. The kitchen is large and roomy, filled with oak and elm cabinets and floors. Glass Mason jars line the shelves filled with dried beans, herbs, tea, flowers, and honey from her bees. The glass jars have traveled with her for many moves. The metal atop them has lost its shine and there are scratches, but it is all these things that make the place feel alive and lived in. The tiles that line her backsplash are hand-painted and feel Celtic. The colors are the greens and blues found in the fields and rivers that flow in her great big backyard.

Reya's master bedroom faces the mountain ridges. There are French doors that open from her room into her backyard. With a café style table and chairs, she created a place to sit and enjoy her tea. There is a small path open to reach the rest of the yard and at the end of it, a trellis and a wall fountain. This place is her sanctuary. She feels safe here and enjoys the time alone.

Inside, her bed is covered with rich blue and soft green

colors. The blankets that accent her sheets are golden yellow. Warm comforters, hand-stitched by her ancestors, lay folded and hanging on a quilt rack near her bedside. The picture that hangs behind her bed is that of an endless view of the sea. The picture made her cry the first time she saw it. She was captivated by the illusion of the never-ending water without any sense of a horizon. Finally, she exhaled when she saw it. For the first time, she felt like someone out there understood her heart. She purchased it immediately and hung it in her room, so she knew she would see it every day when she awoke and before she went to sleep.

Her shower was massive. It was the one indulgence she had to have in her life. A hot shower with excellent water pressure was essential to her ability to function each day. Few things could hold her down or throw her off -center like a cold, wimpy shower. She designed the shower so that it felt like it was outside. She created a space that felt organic, not ornate. She wanted little distance between herself and what lay outside her doors, but she also appreciated fine, simple things. Reya loved organic quality and beauty, not superficial or fake imposters. Accented with lavender and moss colors, the room felt like a spa. The towels were thick and long, rolled up and tied with twine. Her washcloths neatly nestled in a basket on the sink, and her throw rugs were handwoven jute. The soaps in the soap dish were made by hand; an obsession Reya picked up in her travels. She fell in love with handmade soaps created by heartfelt crafters. Buying them made her feel closer to nature while also preserving traditions like these. Each soap had its own personality and scent. She liked to alternate them so her bathroom would smell differently, depending on which soap she selected that day.

There was a spare bedroom for guests and office space, and room to spare, but no one she knew had come to visit her yet.

The unpacked boxes that remained in those rooms were proof of that.

She was at ease with her time alone. Having no visitors felt right. She needed time to get acquainted with her surroundings.

CHAPTER 4
VALO

Her best friend nestles at the foot of her bed and hears her stirring movements. He knows that is his cue to rise. As Reya grabs for a throw, he stretches his massive body and makes a scratching dance as he gazes up at her, his way of telling her he's hungry. His body stands roughly forty inches off the ground. Once hollow from hunger, his torso and chest are now fully formed with a masterful balance of strength and agility. If he stands up on his hind legs, he can easily rest his paws on Reya's shoulders.

"Valo! Come!" she calls him to follow into the kitchen. She preps his breakfast along with hers. His walk is confident and true. With every step, she can see the muscular strength of this creature. His grey and white hair painted by sunlight coming through the kitchen window shimmers like a pearl. Reya rests her hand on his back gently as he walks beside her.

Valo is a mystery just like this place. She believes he is part wolf but is unsure of what else makes up this impressive creature. She tells her friends he's her heart on four legs: not really a dog, just wearing a dog suit for this life. Valo appeared on her doorstep a year before her search for this place began. She was watering a large butterfly bush outside her home when she heard something moving behind the bush. The area was dark, but as she lowered herself to get a better look, she locked eyes with him. Before she ever saw him fully, a surge of energy passed through her from him. It startled and fascinated her. The surprise stunned her with a winded blow. She lost her balance and, as she hit the ground, a flash of golden light came from the space where her eyes had locked on his. The next thing left her speechless as he landed in her lap. His face was battle-worn and his body at the brink of death. His sunken hips and torso told a story Reya didn't want to know. He was starving.

Although she knew instantly he would always be with her, he needed time to know her. She gently coaxed him into the house so she could feed him. The food was gone the second it hit the bowl. Reya was positive he was inhaling, not chewing it. Each morsel she fed him relaxed his shoulders a little bit. When finished with food and water, Valo's eyes expressed gratitude, but fear remained. He walked over to a place on her floor, placed his back against the wall so nothing could approach him without his knowledge, and fell asleep. He slept there for a very long time without movement nor discernible breath. She watched him for a while, wondering what happened to him but, more importantly, how he ended up behind the bush. When he finally woke, she was not in the room. Anxiously searching, he found her in the kitchen making dinner.

"How are you doing?" Reya asked him. He tilted his head back and forth, hanging on her words with curiosity. Reya has had dogs in her life since childhood. She knew how to train them and take care of them. However, she never had a dog that was traumatized. This would be a journey for her, gladly taken for him.

Reya took her time with Valo each day, asking him to trust her a little more. They were intertwined now, knowing that she was a part of his heart. At night, she let him get in bed with her; a habit she had denied her previous dogs. Given his physical state, she wanted to do all she could to make him feel at ease and safe. Each time she touched him, she did it slowly and with intention, so he knew she meant him no harm. He repaid her kindness with loyalty and love beyond any human connection she had experienced. One day, while Reya leaned in to touch his face, he gazed into her eyes and she felt the air shift around her. Then, as if the wind spoke, she heard, "*Valo.*"

"Is that your name boy?"

"Valo," Reya repeated as she stroked his face and nose. His face lifted and he licked her and began to nuzzle his head into her stomach. "I guess that's a yes." From that Moment on, she called him Valo, the most precious of lights she would encounter this lifetime. Reya got down on hands and knees and began nudging him with her head as well. The rest of their lives they would play with each other this way, demonstrating trust and affection in this simple gesture.

CHAPTER 5
BEFORE SOMEWHERE-PREVIOUS HOME

Reya awakened and stared at the wall. She had sensed something or perhaps dreamt something. She wasn't quite sure if it was real. She tried hard to remember what it was, but she couldn't. Frustrated, she couldn't go back to sleep, so she walked downstairs and sat in her backyard for a while. Valo followed her, curious. Reya always felt connected to nature. Walking into it made her feel alert and more alive. Looking up at the stars, she imagined a world beyond her own. She had been waking up a lot since Valo's arrival. She had a new feeling that she was not alone. Her backyard felt like it was moving closer to her. The trees she swore were moving more like they were human than plants. She found herself reaching out to them, talking to them, inquiring whether they could hear or sense her. She would giggle a little and chalk her feelings up to a fantasy.

"Valo, let's go back to bed." Reya walked upstairs and fell asleep again. That night she dreamt her backyard was alive, and the trees were talking to her.

"Come home," they said. "Reya, come home."

Most mornings Reya would awaken and forget all about

what happened the night before. She awoke rested and happy, excited about the day ahead.

Since Valo's arrival, she had begun hiking. The dog's size and nature dictated she keep him active. He made a wonderful hiking companion, walking ahead of her on the trails and then sitting and waiting until she caught up. Initially, she thought this was his way of telling her to hurry, but after a while, she realized Valo was taking her on these hikes. He was trying to show her things she might not see on her own.

Today was like many others, Valo ran ahead of her but when she reached where she thought he would be waiting, he was not.

"Valo, where are you?" she yells. She backtracked her steps to see if she had missed him lying under a tree, but his large size makes this assumption silly, she tells herself. She walks off the trail a little and sees his shimmering fur in the distance, behind a hollowed-out tree. By the looks of it, lightning struck it and charred the bark while killing the roots on impact. Valo is way off the trail. Reya watches her steps for snakes as she makes her way toward him. As she gets closer, she notices he is sitting on something. What is he doing over there?

The last few feet, she realizes that what he is sitting on is man-made. It looks like what remains of a foundation, perhaps the outline of a home which stood here long ago still lingers. There are rocks and bricklike structures that outline the space. There also appears to be a space that is deeper than the spot Valo is sitting on. Is this another room or a cellar? Reya walks the perimeter of what is left and Valo lies down. Reya watches him. He looks peaceful and at home here even though she has never visited this trail before. Following his lead, Reya sits beside her friend and strokes his back. She closes her eyes, enjoying a gentle breeze washing over them. The sun warms her face while her body starts to sway with the rhythm of the trees. She feels an unwinding sensation in her body, a gentle counter-clockwise motion that relaxes her.

Captivated by the energy flowing through her, Reya lets go and sees herself falling forward, off a cliff. At this Moment, she sees a flash of blue light. She doesn't know where it came from, but it shocks her eyes open. As swiftly as it comes, it vanishes, and she is left sitting here in this space that was once a home but is now a memory. A memory, she wondered, if Valo shared? How did he know this place was here? Did he know about the blue lights? Did he feel it, too?

Reya sat in this place a long time before asking Valo to continue with their hike. The pine trees that line the trail along with the huge mountains in the background solidified the idea that this trail was special. Valo and she would visit this spot often over the next few months; always with him running ahead and always with her finding him there, sitting on the foundation, waiting for her.

CHAPTER 6
BEFORE SOMEWHERE-FIRST SYMBOL

Reya's head is pounding. She sits up in bed, finding it is still dark outside. She looks at the clock. It's 3:30 am, her witching hour, again. Lately, she's been waking up often at this time. She rubs her temples and sits on the edge of her bed for a Moment. Standing up to head for the bathroom, she feels the air rush by her. Like the feeling that you get when you open a door, but there is no door here! She feels the floor shake a little but dismisses it. The train must be on its way. Her home does sit near a train track. The shaking gets stronger, adding a roaring sound; a sound the train never makes. It sounds like horses or a herd of buffalo are running through her bedroom. She reaches out as if to touch one running by her, but there is nothing but air. The room is empty yet feels full at the same time. She wants to run with them. She wants to know where they are running.

Come back, she says silently and falls back onto her bed. Did this really happen? The hair on her arms stands up as she feels prickly pins ripple up and down her neck and spine. Reya lays down and falls into a sleep that feels like she is awake, but she knows she isn't. She sees vivid light of white and blue fill her room like stars fill the night's sky. She raises her right hand to touch the air and she feels the air touch her in return.

Her hand, suspended in space without any assistance, is held by a mystery that she longs to know and see. Reya falls asleep with her hand like this. She doesn't remember it falling but when she finally does wake up the next morning her hand is where it should be, on the bed next to her.

Reya has already forgotten about the stampede and her encounter with the bright lights. While pulling off the covers, she notices a symbol on her left pointing finger. Like a tattoo but not really, the color wasn't black or dark but iridescent. Her skin felt raised with an odd texture instead of smooth like a normal tattoo. It looks like a form of writing or perhaps just a design, even a doodle. She doesn't know what it is or what it is for. She licks her fingers and attempts to rub it off. Her efforts prove unsuccessful. She promptly walks to the sink to wash her hand and scrub the symbol with her nail brush, but this, too, fails. A little nervous, she gives up and decides to leave it for now. She takes a towel from the rack and dries her hands. As she wipes them dry, the symbol seems to flatten out and disappear; the outline gone, along with the colors. Reya is no longer able to feel the texture change on her skin, either.

"What the hell is going on?" Reya says with her inside voice. Valo circles her a few times and pulls on her PJs with his teeth. When Reya looks down at him, his eyes are glowing. Reya passes out.

CHAPTER 7

BEFORE SOMEWHERE-SHOWER

W arm sticky saliva dripping in her eyes awakened her. Valo stood over Reya, patiently waiting. When her eyes finally opened, he flattened her with his entire weight while licking her face.

"Oh, my god! Stop it, Valo! I'm fine," Reya says as she pushes him off her. Valo shifts his weight to the side but will not completely stop touching her. Sensing she is not ready to stand yet, he places his front paws on her legs and stares up into her eyes, ensuring that she must sit a little longer. Good thing that he did because Reya feels unraveled and wonders what happened to her.

She looks at her sweet friend and whispers, "Valo, what are you up to?"

Valo looks back innocently, as always, when these things happen. She touches his face, kisses his muzzle, and then lifts herself off the floor.

After taking some time to gather herself, Reya jumps in the shower. As she washes herself, she asks silently what is happening. When she begins rinsing her hair, her hands start to move on their own. They begin to rotate and start making motions and signs. They look like sign language but are more fluid. Reya doesn't know how to sign but as the energy in her hands intensifies, she feels her feet start to move, too. She is dancing to music and making signs with her hands and hasn't one clue why or what it means. More fascinated than afraid, she surrenders to it and her hands turn into weavers of a lovely, unknown language. She enjoys the playful lightness she feels inside while doing it. When she finally gets out of the shower, she notices it lasted twice as long, but it felt as though no time had passed at all during her exploration of this new language.

"Sorry, Valo," she says out loud, "I know you are ready to walk." Reya, happy for this Moment, hurries to dress and head outside.

Her walks with Valo are important and habitual. They were where she first noticed just how unique he is. Valo would pull her toward strangers to meet. Each stranger greeted him with enthusiasm. He would turn and let them pet him while allowing Reya to tell the stranger his story. Now, when Valo enters the park, all the strangers reach out to him regularly, strangers no more. Reya notices she is also no longer a stranger to them and understands that Valo is bringing people closer together just with his presence. Most of her life a loner, Reya is coming out of her shell, talking to others, trusting others yet all the while wishing she could share some of the odd things happening to her at home. She is afraid she will be labeled crazy, out of touch with reality. Given the occurrences of late, she might be inclined to agree with them.

Entering the park feels good. The air is cool on her face, but the sun hot and present. The combined sensation strengthens her, and she encourages Valo to chase her on the trail. As they get farther along on their walk, she hears a whisper: "Sing me a song."

So Reya starts singing to a beat that is coming from the air.

"Inside you are doors that open to access all of
    your gifts. The gifts that lie dormant, awaiting
    your self-discovery. These doors are the colors
    of the rainbow.
"Pick a door and play with me.
"Pick a door and run with me.
"Pick a door and save me.
"Pick a door."

Reya thanked the whisper and returned to walking. This would happen repeatedly on her walks with Valo. Sometimes she would initiate the play by asking the whisper to sing to her. Sometimes the songs would be loving and kind. Other times they were intense and outrageous.

At times, the whisper would contain a brief message or seed of wisdom:

"Sustain is asking yourself to want, be patient,
    and let things come to you naturally."

Or

"In your heart is a pond of unevaporated water
    that is stale and needs refreshing with love
    and kindness to yourself."

Reya didn't realize it, but she was waking up from the inside out. Like light switches on the wall, Reya was flipping internal switches and liking the electricity. She didn't know where the voice or whisper came from, like most things in her life now. She was accessing things without an operating manual; a feeling of wonder accompanying these times. Amazing as they were, she questioned why they were happening to her and what she ultimately was supposed to do with it all.

CHAPTER 8
BEFORE SOMEWHERE -
CHANGING

O ver the past eight months, Valo guided Reya on many hikes and some contained a sacred nugget of play with nature. Still self-conscious about the happenings in her mind and body, she once again began to isolate herself from others. She found the things she was feeling and dreaming about more fascinating than the people in her life. She felt torn inside. On one hand, she loved her home and her yard and knew so many wonderful happenings in her space. There was also an unsettled part of her that wanted to discover more about the world and herself in it. She didn't feel like she belonged in the neighborhood anymore. Her friends, dear and loving, felt like strangers to her. She found herself bored in conversations with them. It wasn't their fault. Often, she intuited what they were going to say before they said it. She heard them start the same stories over and over and worried that she might do the same, like a hamster stuck on a wheel going nowhere fast. Reya wanted off the wheel. Reya didn't want to be a hamster at all.

When her friends inquired about her life, Reya struggled to share anything, as all her thoughts had to do with her new sacred space. She thought her friends might be bored with her, too. When she stared at them across a lunch table or entering their home, Reya started feeling like they were strangers. Their eyes didn't look the same anymore. The recognition disappeared and she started feeling lost inside spaces that once felt like home. She didn't trust that they would understand her. Uncertain that she wouldn't be judged or declared mentally incompetent, she kept the mysteries to herself.

In time Reya stopped reaching out to her friends altogether. Except for a rare few, Reya spent most of her days with Valo and Valo alone.

She had no idea that hearing that first whisper would change her so much. She didn't realize she'd become sensitive to so many other things around her. Her perspective of things began to shift. All the things she thought she had a grasp on were altering with each interaction. She had heard of spiritual awakenings and wondered if this is what is meant by that.

If waking up meant death. Not a physical death but the death of your reality, knowledge, and criticisms about the world. Each day Reya was waking up and rewriting what she thought was true the day before. Things that used to get her really upset appeared trivial. Things and places that once brought her joy no longer sparked her interest nor time.

Time itself felt different now to Reya. She noticed how some things occupied more time and space while others were just blips. She wondered how time played so much of a role in her life. Hiking with Valo and playing with time changed this for her. It was a game of stretching and snapping back.

"Who plays with time?" she asked herself. The more she played, the weirder she felt. This weirdness grew into a desire to change herself entirely.

The invitation from the voice to "Come home," pulled her soul. There was a delicious seduction in it, not because her life was lacking but because of the delight that came with each invi-tation, a feeling of wholeness or community. Like when you visit your best friend and relax to be who you are with them. No pretenses or defenses, simply friendship.

CHAPTER 9
BEFORE SOMEWHERE -
MEDITATION

I n her backyard is Reya's favorite place to meditate. The
freshness and openness make it a natural place to unwind.
Hummingbirds circle the red feeder hanging from the lemon
tree saturated with delicate white flowers. Each one attempts to
outmaneuver the other. The buzzing signals the birds' inbound
attempts to perch on the feeder and drink the sugar water first.
Frequently the hummingbirds announce themselves by putting
on an airshow. They look like miniature fighter pilots in a dog
fight rolling and zipping by her.

River rocks line the yard, giving the illusion that a river
flows over the grass. The rise and fall of the rocks along with
their different colors give the space depth and warmth. At
night, solar lights parallel the river. Glistening rocks shimmer
like water tempting anyone to put their toe in to touch the
temperature. Three large pine trees monitor her activity from
on high. Trees standing over twenty years see Reya and wonder
if she sees them. They send her signals, but they are unsure if
she receives them. They are accustomed to this time with her
and love when she comes over to speak to them directly. She

bows in front of them periodically, and they are touched by her warm heart.

Reya relaxes. The dark brown rattan chair has a high back and large armrests. The cushion she sits on is plush and larger than usual, for comfort. Meditating requires discipline but distractions can affect the experience. Reya didn't want an uncomfortable chair to interfere so she makes the chair and her surroundings as distraction-free as possible.

Breathing in and out with intention, Reya places her earbuds in her ears and presses play on her phone. A recent download from the spa channel sets the mood. She begins her voyage inward.

"Inhale."

"Exhale."

"Inhale, deeper this time."

"Exhale, slowly."

The music infiltrates her muscles and bones and the tissue on her melts into her shoulders like little pools of lava flowing along a scorched Earth. Her hands rest on top of her legs, but after several minutes her palms got so hot, the skin underneath was red from the warmth. Slowly and methodically, Reya's body began moving. With each movement her spine stacked perfectly in alignment, starting from her hips up to her head. This took time and with each shift, she felt afraid and excited. Her body moved subtly in the shower but never like this with such intensity. When energetic force got to her head, it gently tilted her head and opened her mouth. Her mouth opened so wide she felt her jaw might snap.

Then a rod of lightning pushed into Reya's mouth past her throat. Struck by a force so powerful, she was held in place for a while. Jaw open, energy pushing further into her with the power of lightning and thunder and all the elements combined. The force traveled through the center of her body and out the floor. Although she saw nothing in the room, the experience was real.

After what seemed eternity to her, the force, as if sensing her body reached its limits, left. Reya slid out of the chair to the ground and crawled back into her home. Valo, whimpering, pacing, and watching Reya, struggled to stand up. Hugging the walls and leaning on Valo, Reya makes her way to her bedroom and falls into bed. She thinks she's having a heart attack and the top of her head feels hot to touch. Her head singed, her body on fire, and her insides feel like a thousand horses are running through her intestines. She is unsure if she should call a doctor or go to the ER. Valo sensing her needs hops on the bed and tries to calm her. He rests his head on her hand, a distraction from the physical stress. Valo lays calmly inches closer to Reya so that she feels the calm rhythm of his breath. Reya's breathing slowly now matches his. The soft constant in and out creates a cocoon around them both. Her spirit leaves her physical body floating above her watching her and Valo sleep. She realizes that this part of her is the part that is connected to the unexplainable events happening in her life. She feels an amazing sense of love flowing between her and Valo as well as around her. She knows now that this indescribable experience has changed her cellularly forever. She senses that the symbols and flashes of light are breadcrumbs leading her on a journey that is not ready to reveal itself to her yet. Until this latest occurrence, she never felt like anything bad could happen to her, but this last episode was the most powerful things she'd ever felt. It almost felt like a warning. Warning her that one, if she continued there was no going back and two, if she weren't ready her body could not hold the sacred downloads no matter how much she wanted to continue. As she feels her physical body signal it's time for her to return, she catches a glimpse of three majestic mountains. She's never seen them before but instantly she wants to be where they are. Her chest opens to swallow the image keeping it safe for her to revisit. Revisit the feeling they gave her and the determination that came with it to find them.

CHAPTER 10
SOMEWHERE-HOME

In between unpacking boxes and organizing her new life, Reya mapped out several hikes for Valo and her to explore. She wanted to explore the land that drew her here. The mountains specifically. She believed they called to her and she wanted to discover the reasons behind it.

Her property, although humble, had the best view. The fields behind her home were filled with wildflowers and various tall grass. She gained a sensation of vast freedom looking at it. The trees stood like observers over fields, but also gatekeepers to the three mountains beyond them. The fields felt alive with riddles about living nature and how it attempts to interact and play with us. Reya felt like moving here in this specific spot was magical. She never imagined her life would end up so simple and beautiful yet filled with mystery and fascination.

Today she would set out to hike to the first ridge on the left. She filled the Camelback bladder with water and packed the essentials: snacks, first aid kit, flint, warming blanket, duct tape, and rope. She also grabbed her hiking poles along with Valo's pack. She used his pack for extra water and food. She was always cautious to prepare for anything. Since no one else lived with her, she knew she had to be careful and prepared to handle any circumstance on her own. She carried a cell phone, but coverage was spotty. Mostly the phone was to take pictures and record things that came to mind while she walked.

Valo is pacing because he knows when she grabs the poles, they are headed out to play. He is excited and pushes his hip against her thigh. His eyes widen and he investigates hers as if talking directly to her. "Almost time to go boy," Reya pats his head to calm him but he will not settle until he crosses to the outside.

Reya glances at herself in the mirror before she reaches for the handle of the front door. She feels nervous inside with excitement and anticipation. This will be her first venture out beyond that sanctuary she calls home. Her expectations are high, and she hopes this is the first day in a series of many which will reveal the rest of the story her heart longs to write.

As she secures her hat and glances at the woman in the mirror, she touches her chiseled hair. Lately, it has been breaking off on the ends more. The breaks are hard and appear to be making a pattern of chaos. Geometrically it works she thinks but it also concerns her because she cannot stop it. Each angle of the break is precise as if scissors did it, but she hasn't cut her hair since she moved. Finding a hairstylist is the last thing on her mind. The most curious thing about it is that when the hair breaks, she hears it breaking. She touches the ends, and they look like jagged diamonds but also feel like ice water. She shakes her head and ponders over the phenomena and then says to herself, "Something else to think about while I'm walking."

Valo on the brink lets out a howl and Reya knows there is no more time to wait. She opens the front door. Valo runs out with an enthusiasm that fills her with joy. It wasn't long ago that he barely played or showed any signs of excitement. Now he looks wild and free and whole like the essence he was meant to be.

The door closes behind her and she hears a whisper deep within. "Go to the meadow and find them." Her left shoulder glows under her shirt. She doesn't see it glowing, but she feels it awaken. There is no ignoring it even though she'd like to. The whisper will get louder if she does. All she wanted was today to explore and now she is being given directions by a symbol. "Fine" she reluctantly says to herself. "Have it your way."

CHAPTER 11
GLIMPSE INTO THE UNKNOWN

Clear liquid light moves around and around, tracing infinity symbols.
Edges outlined in yellow-gold lights.
Transparent yet visible.
The liquid endlessly highlights infinity in the air and the air in the infinity.
Eyes close.
Eyes open.
Liquid light remains.

CHAPTER 12
SOMEWHERE – THE MEADOW

The organic meadow that lay outside her property felt never-ending. The high grasses were plentiful. A painter's pallet of corn yellow, hunter's and vermillion green, olive, and wintergreen abundant as far as the eye can see. Speckled throughout were hints of lilac, burnt umber, crimson red, and deep orange. An artist's utopia, the landscape held her gaze as she took time to pass her hand over the blades of grass gently. With each touch of her hand to an individual blade of grass, a daring sense of knowing came to her that an amazing force lives in the soil below her feet. A rich garden of love, loss, hope, and desolation. A garden of life and death and all the properties in between. This soil held the stories of the ancient ones who lived here before Reya. The stories of each plant sacrificing itself to the soil, each animal contributing to the landscape that lies below and each skeleton giving back so that the soil enriches over time. The stories untold to her or anyone else fester below the soil, waiting to be called. Instead, the stories became echoes buried deep within the soil. Stories waiting to be discovered; kept by the Unknown and released when required. The individual blades of grass were babies birthed from the soil, birthed from the echoes, and birthed from the Earth itself. They were infants and toddlers and even teenagers. They felt tender and kind and held a desire for her touch and blessing. These were alive but unlike plants Reya had related to in the past. She knew plants were living on a cellular level. Everyone in school had to take biology and botany. But she had never associated grass with an eye that resembled herself. The grass had feelings, and they were feeling her, too, and she felt overcome with this recognition. In the distance, the mountains stood, watching Reya. She glanced at them, understanding she would not make the hike to them today, but she didn't mind spending more time here. In fact, she needed to stay and gain more insight. Reya looked at Valo and said, "Go play." He sprinted away from her, tearing off through the field, jumping and rolling around. She decided to place her backpack on the ground as a pillow. Leaning back and into the field, she felt the leaves welcome her. The moisture remaining from the dew cooled her. The grounding effect felt familiar while the smell of musk and fungus gently touched her nose. She wanted to talk to the leaves and the grass, imagining they might sit up and tell her all their secrets. While lying there, looking into the sky, a nurturing feeling came over her, and she slipped into a dream-like space.

Watching in the background, the mountains Viime and Tulevaisuus stand up and switch places. They are playing a game. Often when one of them sleeps the others will move and wait to see if the one sleeping will notice upon waking.

Dreaming.

Oblivious, Reya sees the plants alive with love, faces, talents, and abilities far beyond what she understood them to have. Seeds began to encircle her. They had different edges and textures and smells. Some were smooth and tiny while others looked like little beings with faces. Astonished, she could see the little beings in the seeds and smell them, too. They dispersed exotic and familiar fragrances from all over the world. They were vibrant seeds with little seedlings blooming out of them while floating on the air in front of her. The seeds were humming and pulsating and with each vibration, her fingers began to scrawl symbols in the earth, each movement precise and with intention. An intention not coming from her mind but from her spirit, her soul, or perhaps her heart. With each marking, the seeds responded. They would spring forth new leaves or sprouts and smells. Reya was sure that these symbols were a natural outpouring. She was connecting to the meadow as children connect to each other: with innocence and exploration and without judgements or agendas. Time stood still for Reya and the meadow. The saplings sent a ripple into the Unknown and the Unknown returned the ripple as a wave of happiness. A happiness that forces a smile from inside Reya. Her face and lips light up, and she can't control the edges of her mouth. Extending to the fullest angle possible, she smiles for the first time from the inside, the lines in her eyes and cheeks deep and taught; her eyes bright and her body alert.

Reya sits up refreshed. Glancing down for just a Moment she notices several symbols raise and then lower back into her skin. The shimmering light disappearing along with them.

Several hours passed during this exchange and Valo was the one to bring Reya back. He was hungry and pulling on her hiking pants to tell her as much. Her stroll back home was quiet. Even the meadow felt still. She didn't hear a bird chirp, nor a cricket, nor even a bee buzz by. She felt a stillness that extended from inside of her out toward the meadow. The more she questioned it, the more distracted she became and just like that the silence broke. The sounds of nature came rushing in like a wave, as though the door opened this morning inviting, her here. She heard that door close, and the whisper returned with a "Thank you." Reya placed her hand on her heart and said, "You are always welcome in my heart."

Later that evening, Reya fell asleep quickly. Her visit to the meadow left her relaxed and vulnerable. She felt like anything that ever happened to her in the past was ready to wash away with a deep, deep sleep.

Dreaming.

Reya opens a glass door and walks into a space filled with a beautiful, blinding white light. After a Moment, she can see them: a circle of viewers. She doesn't know who they are. Are they angels or ancient beings? She doesn't recognize any of their faces. No matter how many times she attempts to speak to them, no words come out. She feels them looking at her and they are smiling. She wants so badly to reach out and touch them. The circle begins to fade, along with the viewers. She blinks, and the circle, once filled with beings, is replaced by a full moon, glowing with a pink hue around its circumference. Reya reaches out to touch it. Almost there, she stands as tall as she can and stretches out her arm, but her fingers just miss their mark. The moon slips away, and she feels lost. She wants the viewers to return to her. She wants them to share who they are and why they came to visit her. Reya returns to the door she had entered, but the handle is different. Once a handle, it is now a bright canary yellow flower. She pushes the door open and a warm breeze blows her back gently. She sees fields and fields of flowers, as far as the eye can see. Tulips and daisies, violets and orchids stand softly moving in the breeze. Reya is not a botanist, but she knows it would be odd for all of these plants to grow together in one field, but she does not care. It is breathtaking. The smell of roses fills the air along with sweet nectar. She touches the tulips and honey drips from the petals. She places her fingers in her mouth to taste blackberries and thyme. Her heart feels at home, yet her mind keeps repeating that this must be a dream. The flowers are emitting little lights from their petals and stems. The lights leave one flower and fly to another and each time, the flowers respond by releasing a different colored light. Reya observes this happening all over the field. When she understands what is happening, the lights stop. The flowers are talking to each other, she thinks. They are sharing information and understandings about their surroundings. The lights turn as if looking directly at her. Moving like choreographed dancers, they hover in front of Reya. She extends her arms and turns her wrists, palms up, in hopes they might land on her hands. As her palms flatten, the lights fly straight up and dive directly into her palms, each light shifting into a seed, sapling, bud, or flower bloom. She feels the lights travel into her body, her mind, and her heart. Once the last light enters her palm, she finds herself back at the door with the flower handle. As the door shuts behind her, a voice says, "Wake up!"

Reya's eyes shot open wide, looking around to see who said that. Valo lifted his head and stared at her. With a concerned look, he wanted to know what she was doing. Reya patted his head a couple of times to tell him that everything is fine.

CHAPTER 13
SOMEWHERE – THE FOREST

After Reya's visit in the meadow, she couldn't shake a burning desire to plant a small garden. Feeling closer and closer to nature, she thinks it would be a nice way to keep her fascination with the meadow alive

Reya spreads some homemade blackberry jam on toast and methodically dunks a sachet of fine oolong tea leaves into a ceramic mug. She loves the smell of the delicate leaves combined with the rustic smell of toast. She cups her warm mug in both hands to let the steam and natural scent of earth touch her face. She leans against the kitchen sink to eat her breakfast today. It's helping her think and wake up.

While she contemplates gardening and what that might look like, she starts packing to hike. She is going to the mountains today, so she packs extra snacks for Valo, extra water, and sunscreen. She also thinks a flashlight might be in order because she is going through the forest and is unsure how dense and dark the canopy might be. Holding the rest of the toast between her teeth, blackberry juice dripping from her lips and chin, she hops on one foot while forcing the other into a hiking boot. The rugged Vibram soles protect her feet from sharp edges and thorns and are great for long treks or just clearing a path through tangled bushes.

With Valo already waiting at the front door, Reya steps to the door and turns her head to glance into the mirror. She doesn't know why she does this. It feels natural to see herself before she leaves. Like a private conversation or acknowledgement, she feels compelled to take a second to pause before she departs. Today, as she turns to look, she sees a pale yellow-green light radiating from her head. She pauses to stare at the sight while reaching forward to touch the mirror. Perhaps something is on the mirror, she thinks, as she rubs her sleeve over her reflection. She steps back and looks again. Her reflection is now replaced by a hand, looking very much like her hand, with symbols on it. It begins pushing its fingers through the glass and into her space, stopping just beyond the border of the frame that outlines the glass. A mound of dirt rises from just a few bits of dust in the palm of the hand. Reya, mesmerized, wants to scream but her breath is trapped in her lungs.

The mound begins to spin counterclockwise and a small tree pushes up from the dirt mound. The tree is an English oak or elm; she is unsure which. The tree spins until it looks like a miniature mature tree, growing from the center of the hand. The tree stops and Reya's body begins to bow. She doesn't know why or how but her body is bowing to the tree. When the action is complete, the tree starts spinning again but faster this time. As the speed intensifies, the tree dissolves into a million grains of wheat, barley, and rice. A wave of grains come toward her and then disperse into the air. She watches the grains float and then explode into little stars, creating fireworks in front of her eyes. She tries to move to touch them, but she is still frozen, not breathing, eyes dilated, and logic blown away, attempting to comprehend. Once the hand retreats into the mirror, her lungs release. She falls forward against the mirror. She looks at the space where the hand was and pulls the mirror away from the wall to look behind it. Silly, she knows, but a natural reflex given the circumstances. Valo, instead of his usual impatient pacing, innocently sits in the yard, staring at Reya. Perhaps Valo knows what is happening and is patiently waiting for her to catch up.

She tells him, "You could have given me a heads-up." Valo barks twice and turns around. He is ready to hike and that's all there is to it.

Reya walks through the meadow and heads toward the tree line. Inside she hears the blades of grass greeting her. They sway a little quick sachet when she touches them and then resume their normal cadence in the wind. Tickled, Reya talks to the meadow.

"Oh, meadow of all meadows, you are a delight to walk through.
I cherish seeing you here and love that you are home to so many
delicate things.
I love you, little wild rose.
I love you, little crickets.
I love you, little wild currants.
I love you, little ladybugs.
I love you," she whispers.

Reya walks on, gently stepping on the grass with a new tenderness in her feet. Approaching the edge of the forest, she sees a border of mountain sage bushes with chokecherry growing alongside and weaving in between. The wise sage stands at just about four feet while the lovely cream-like flowers with buttery yellow centers of the chokecherry easily stand ten feet tall, offering an ornate entrance for whomever might enter. Not unlike a welcome mat at the front door. The forest is welcoming Reya to visit. Her senses tell her again she will not make it to the mountains today, but she surrenders with a sigh, shifting her focus to the deep, rich forest that stands before her.

CHAPTER 14
THE TREE

Upon clearing the entryway, Reya presents herself to a 30-foot-tall quaking Aspen who is flanked by his family born from his roots. The other Aspens vary in size and height, standing with the strength of their father flowing through them. In unison, the leaves quake, and a ripple pulsates from the ground up through Reya's feet. A surge of strength grounds her to the Earth almost as if her feet have become roots. She interprets this as the feeling the Aspens have, rooted here. Deep love is here; she senses it. A love of time and commitment to the Earth. A vast love that doesn't feel personal but more nurturing, like a safety net or a mother's hand outstretched to her young child. A love that is held by nature, in nature, for nature.

Reya walks over to the father Aspen and places her hand on the smooth white bark. The tree, longing to be recognized and touched for many years, erupts with happiness.

"A gift from me to you," she hears it whisper to her.

"What gift?" Reya responds. In that instant, her hands move in front of her toward each other. The three middle fingers give each other a tap on the tips and circle around to do it again. The thumb and the pinkie finger extend out while the three repeat this round after round after round. Aspen joins in by sending a root up that encircles her hands. The roots are massaging her wrists and leaving behind symbols that flicker in green light, then dissolve.

Inside her heart, Reya hears, "I am Veli, and these are my children. We are the sentries that stands guard over the entrance to the forest."

Each of his children bends toward Reya slightly. "All of my children are connected to me. No one nor thing can enter here without all of us knowing it. We are the perfect messengers to alert the forest to those who enter. When one of us is harmed, we are all harmed." Reya looks at all of them and nods.

"Is this the best way to get to the three mountain ridges beyond the forest?" Reya asks.

"Yes, it is, but before you see the mountains, you must first visit with Aiti," Veli says.

"Aiti, who is Aiti?" Reya responds.

"Aiti is the mother of the forest. She is the keeper of all wisdom and knowledge among the trees and, unlike the rest of us, is from a space and time unknown."

As Veli talks with Reya, she gently strokes his bark and then visits his children, touching them, too. No matter how far she gets from Veli, she hears him in her heart. One after another, she strokes the Aspens, and they respond with little quakes. As Veli shares with Reya, she ponders what he meant by the Unknown.

"How do I see this Aiti?" Reya asks Veli.

"She lives in the deepest part of the forest. Take your time. We have sent word that you are coming. Don't worry, sweet girl, you will be protected by the trees and the animals which live here. Enjoy the journey and remember to listen."

"Listen to what?" Reya asks.

"To all the creatures who live here, each one divine and with purpose. The creatures of this forest are of time's remembrance. They are not just animals; they are also the images of life after life."

Valo, as if alerted by a call or a whistle, jumps to his feet and heads into the forest. The entire time Reya spoke to the Aspen, he lay in front of them. He did not visit the Aspen with her. He waited until he was permitted to escort her onward. Valo is excited to see Aiti and excited for Reya.

Reya, confused by Veli's last words, decides that questions could come later. She strokes her new friend one last time before walking forward into the forest.

Reya walks about 500 feet and realizes she can no longer see the Aspens. She is surrounded by an ocean of trees. Warm vanilla and butterscotch hang on the air, dripping into her senses. Her body responds to the smell, "Aww, this place smells yummy, Valo."

Valo chases a squirrel who teased him. The trees are as endless as the waves in the ocean. She doesn't quite know where Aiti is nor how far she must walk to find her, but in the meantime, she is loving the sounds and smells. The Ponderosa pines envelop her, and she thinks that if living outside smells this good, she just might have to live here in the woods. Reya recognizes the power of the smell.

She is transported at this Moment to an ice cream shop. She feels her mother's hand touching her, coaxing her to pick a flavor. Reya wants all the flavors. Settling on just one, Reya chooses a vanilla ice cream cone with butterscotch sprinkles. She can hear her mother and feels her presence here now with her. She is reminded fondly of her mother's love and she sits with this experience for a while.

Coming back from the daydream with shoulders chilled and cool hands, Reya grabs her fleece from her backpack. She can still see the sun between the trees, but the air feels suddenly cooler.

Out of the corner of her eye, she sees wings, green and rust-colored wings, surrounding her head. They are juniper hairstreak butterflies with halos of pink light surrounding them. Reya doesn't ever recall seeing butterflies with luminous auras. A few of them land on her fleece and look up at her. She stands very still, admiring them. Delicate, she tells herself, to refrain from touching them. They only stay a second and then fly in front of her, lighting a path ahead. As they fly farther from her, a runway into the forest is lit by the butterflies.

I must be getting closer to Aiti, Reya thinks.

The dense woods now resemble her backyard at night when lit by lanterns and the fire pit. The butterflies reveal a hidden sacred circle. The circle of six trees includes alternating Japanese maple and pink weeping cherry trees. The site is spectacular. The pink and red leaves lit by the butterflies give the illusion that the air around the trees is on fire. A large, moss-covered rock stands in front of each tree. The ground around the circle is soft like marshmallows. In the center of the circle stands a giant dragon's blood tree. Six large branches weave upward toward the sky. Topped with green leaves, the tree resembles a large canopy or umbrella. Reya is astonished to see eyes in the bark of the tree. Small droplets of what appears to be blood are dripping from the would-be eyes.

A voice speaks to Reya's heart, "You look beautiful, child. I've been waiting for you."

Reya understands that this tree is Aiti, the mother of the forest. "Waiting for me? Why?" Reya asks.

"Because you are the caretaker of the seeds. The Unknown has been awaiting your arrival. Come, sit down inside the circle and invite Valo to sit with you."

"All right," Reya responds, stepping lightly into the circle along with Valo. The butterflies disperse. Yellow and white flowers with blue lights in the center of each open at the top of

Aiti. The air that once looked like fire looks like the northern aurora borealis.

"Sit here and share some time with me," Aiti responds.

Reya and Aiti continue to communicate telepathically. Valo watches their faces as they express themselves for a while until the lights on the tree start to dim. Then Reya curls up under the limbs of this dear tree and slips into a deep sleep. Valo, protective, curls up next to her.

Valo sleeps until Reya, now awakened, strokes his back. He jumps up, wags his tail, and pushes his head into her, waiting for her to do the same. Reya returns the affection and assures him she is fine. She stretches, brushes off her clothes and hair, and stretches her hand to touch Aiti, promising, "I will visit again soon."

Reya and Valo walk back to her home. On their return, they are greeted intermittently by hawks, eagles, mountain lions, and two baby bear cubs. None of the animals get remarkably close. They stepped into her line of sight, allowing just enough time for her to see them. The animals are wild, and this is their home. Reya respects that. Mostly she wants them to know that she will not harm them because the forest belongs to them. She is grateful they allowed her to visit Aiti.

Saying a final goodbye to Veli, Reya steps into the meadow. The ground begins to shake. Frightened, she thinks that it's an earthquake. She grabs Valo tightly and starts to head back into the forest for protection, but her feet are rooted in the earth. It's the same energy she had felt in the forest holding her in place now. Unable to move, Reya sees a herd of horses running from the far edge of the meadow toward her. The sound is deafening. Her insides shake and her left hand tangles Valo's hair, holding on for dear life. The power of the herd rushes by her, but still, she is frozen. She closes her eyes. They part around her as if she were a boulder or tree in the way. She can smell their sweat and feel their breath. They are so close that their passing blows her hair toward her cheeks. Once they are past, she opens her eyes. The ground barely shaking now, Reya gasps. A slight whiff of the horses' scent is the only proof that they were ever there. In a flash, she is transported back to "before somewhere" in her bedroom when she felt the same sensation as now. Remembrance shatters the boundaries of her reality.

Reya starts to cry, drops trickling down her cheeks. Legs quivering as they loosen from whatever hold she was in. She wipes the tears from her eyes and looks down to find her fingers are blood red. The same blood red as the dragon blood tree. Reya's hand begins to move. Her index finger, wet with sap from the tree, begins making a "V" in between her eyes. The sticky sap smells sweet. Reya draws her finger close to her lips, tempted to lick her fingers. As she opens her mouth to taste the stickiness, the sap fades from her finger.

VIIME AND TULEVAISUUS, THE MOUNTAINS, ARE POUNDING ON THEIR CHESTS, TRYING TO WAKE LASNA.

Dreaming:

Reya feels like she is floating in the air. A beautiful city comes into view. A rainbow skyline of tall buildings fills the airy space. The city is floating above the Earth. She can see the blue sky and clouds and feel the wind on her face.

"Wait, how can I feel the wind if I am dreaming?" she observes to herself. This is not a space station or Mars. It looks like someone uprooted a regular city, placed booster rockets underneath, and pushed it to hover in the air. Fascinated with the view, Reya's perspective shifts to deeper within the city. There is a vehicle ahead. Like an observer inside the car, Reya can see the passengers. A mother is talking to her little girl,

sitting in the passenger seat. She appears about five or six years old. Her eyes look like blue marbles with clouds in them. Honey gold rings surround her irises. She is telling her mom something. She looks so inno-cent and wide-eyed. For a Moment, Reya feels like the little girl can see her. The fright of this possibility ends the dream. Reya awakens with a jolt.

CHAPTER 15
RECOVER AND REALIZE

Weeks had passed since Reya met Aiti. The introduction took a lot out of her mentally and physically. She did not understand why she felt so tired, but she and Valo stayed close to home while she nurtured herself back to full strength. She slept all day sometimes, only waking to eat and sit outside with Valo. Her dreams were vivid and expansive. She often felt like she was wide awake instead of dreaming. She felt a cosmic shift inside her body. It felt simultaneously unnerving and exhilarating. When she looked out her windows in the morning, she felt like she was looking at the world through clearer lenses. The sky, the horizon, looked brighter and alive. Some days they would walk to the meadow and have lunch. She would bring along a bed roll so that Valo could play while she watched. Valo was patient with her and let her recuperate. Reya apologized to him daily, feeling guilty about her sudden energy loss, but Valo loved Reya and stayed close, ensuring she felt safe and supported during this vulnerable time.

Lying in the meadow, Reya questioned if perhaps Aiti transferred to her a form of wisdom that could not be spoken nor processed like an instruction manual. The exchange of energy affected her cellularly. She did not know how, but she knew that she felt different than before her walk in the forest.

CHAPTER 16
GLIMPSE INTO THE UNKNOWN

Acrystal Pyramid suspended in dark infinite space
Transparent, yellow and white light emanating around and through
Perspective, challenged by motion
One single seed remains centered, unaffected
Opposite perspectives collapse into and through each other, taking the
place of the other for eternity

CHAPTER 17
SEEDS

S he selected Lilac & Buttercup soap for her shower this morning. Drawn to it, she did not question her choice. She turned on the shower and let the water flow over her. The soap opened her senses. The curious combination eased her achy joints and offered her aromatic comfort. After she inhaled the soap's fragrance a little longer, she set it down in a bamboo soap dish and grabbed for her sponge. Suddenly, as if alive, her hands began to move. First, her right hand gently caresses her left forearm, then moves up to her shoulder. The symbols, dormant underneath her skin, lit up as she hovered over them. Her hand then moved toward her neck slightly over her left breast where it began to make small circles in a counterclockwise motion. Her right hand did this several times and then her left hand started the same sequence over and over. When she finished, her hands came together in front of her like they are going to pray, but only the heel of her hand and the fingertips touched, leaving space between the palms. The space looks like a leaf. She held this movement while her thumbs began to tap each other on the insides of the thumbs then push out and circle back to do it again. She giggles and reaches for her shampoo.

Feeling refreshed from her shower, Reya decided to go to town to stock up on supplies. Her cabinets were getting empty and she was itching to take a drive to get out of the house for a time. She opened the door to her Expedition and Valo climbed in. Pacing back and forth in the back seat, Valo is ecstatic they are taking a ride.

Driving back from town, Reya stopped at a local farmer's fruit and vegetable truck parked near the main road. One of her favorite things to do, Reya loved to buy fresh produce because she did it as a child with her grandmother. The stand looked new. It was clean and sparkling, not like the normally scratched and dirty vegetable trucks she was used to. So distinctive that she mentioned it to the owner.

"Your truck looks brand new," she said.

"Oh, this thing. No, she is not new. I just take really good care of her," the owner remarked.

"My name is Reya. I live a few miles from here."

"I'm Kuriiri. Pleased to meet you, Reya. Look around and let me know if you need any help."

She took her time looking at the ripe berries. Reya enjoyed picking out fresh produce. She wanted to have the most pleasurable tastes from her food. Eating was an experience that she lived for. She wanted the food to be an extension of her heart's expression about loving life, herself, and experiencing the richness and sensuousness found in food, and in all things, really. Gently she stroked the fruit like touching a lover. Freshness oozed off the bins and baskets.

"What is this?" Reya asked when she spotted little brown paper envelopes with markings on each. The envelopes were approximately the size of a 3X5 notecard. These plain, inconspicuous little envelopes had grabbed Reya's attention, and now she could not take her eyes off them. She closed her eyes a little as her hand neared the envelope closest to her. Her fingertips started buzzing. As she picked up the envelope, she saw in her mind's eye a little sprout shoot out of the ground and flex its tiny leaves. A small grin formed on the left side of her mouth, raising toward a full smile when Kuriiri rounded the stand and asked Reya if she needs any assistance.

Startled, she looks at him, asking, "What's inside these little envelopes?"

"Oh, those are seeds," he says.

"What kind of seeds?"

"Different kinds from everywhere."

Kuriiri tells her how he likes to collect them and trade them with other farmers. He explains to her that many are considered heirloom seeds. Growers collect different variants of vegetables and fruit to preserve the species. Families of farmers for generations have saved and preserved seeds, like history, passed down generationally so their families might have a piece of their lineage and understand it through food. Changes in climate along with commercial farming stifled the freedom for growing heirloom species, large farms opting instead for focused efficient farming.

Fascinated, she looked at him, concentrating on every word.

"The envelopes don't have labels on them. How do you know what seeds are in them?" Reya questioned.

Kuriiri says to her, smiling. "You don't. You just trust you've selected the right one for you." An odd response she thought, but her fingers were buzzing, and she knew something about what he said was true even though it made no logical sense.

"Do you have a favorite?" she asks.

"No, but did you know there are thousands of types of beans?" Kuriiri added.

Reya continued. "I love beans, but how do you pick a favorite out of thousands?"

"I want to try them all. Whenever I get a chance to experience something new, I do it."

Reya, dumbfounded that there were so many species of

beans, almost forgot why she stopped at the stand.

"I'll take one of each envelope," she says, "along with those berries and that swiss chard."

"What do the symbols on the envelopes mean?" she asks.

Kuriiri looks at her with curiosity. "Symbols?" He looked puzzled. "Oh, that may be the manufacturer's trademark, I guess."

Reya started to say that is not what she meant but realized he possibly didn't see the symbols on them. So instead, she shook her head and dropped the subject.

Kuriiri totaled up her purchases and placed her items in the recycled bag she handed him.

On her drive home, Valo sat up front with Reya. She felt happy for no reason except that her meeting with Kuriiri stimulated her curiosity. She could hardly wait to open the seeds and plant them.

After dinner, Reya sat in bed and read one of the books stacked on her nightstand. Bookmarks stick arbitrarily out of various books. She likes to keep a stack of them nearby. She often starts one and stops it for a while then begins another and so on.

She scans the stack and wishes she had some books about plants or flowers. In the past, Reya has found her "inner gardener" lacking. Not for lack of desire, but perhaps a lack of focus or patience. She reached for her tablet instead and searched for "heirloom seeds." The search returned 13.4 million hits. "Holy crap!" Reya thought to herself.

She clicked on a link at random, https://www.magicgardenseeds.com/

She read the company's description and scrolled through the menu. Reya loved that the company was dedicated to preserving "biodiversity." She didn't fully understand it but thought it had something to do with organic versus hybrid or genetically modified foods.

She spent several hours looking at sites and fell asleep with her tablet on her chest.

VIIME AND TULEVAISUUS SWITCH PLACES AND WAIT TO SEE HOW LONG IT TAKES FOR LASNA TO NOTICE.

Dreaming:

Potted plants rest on top of shelves. White clean shelves. Too clean, she thought. The white walls and the white shelves and the bright lights magnified the deep rich colors of each plant. Reya felt the importance of this place but did not know where it was. As she strained to see inside the room, she felt a coolness. A rich, calming force came over her in the dream.

This place was special, and she thought "I just need to see a little more to identify where it is."

As if watching a movie, the camera pans to the left and she sees rows and rows of drawers. Drawers labeled with unfamiliar remarks and phrases. The writing is unclear in the dream, but she thinks she catches a quick glimpse of one drawer that is labeled Take Your Time. *Perplexed, Reya continues her tour of the space. The camera speeds up like someone pushed "fast forward" on a video. She sees thousands of seeds along with plants and flowers. She sees sachets and bottles filled with tinctures and then as the movie slows down, she hears a voice say "Anushka."*

The movie stops and just like that Reya is back in her bed, wide awake. It is 3:30 a.m. and she is filled with awe and inspiration. She wants to know more about this place where the plants are growing and who is growing them. Maybe this person could help her learn how to grow the seeds she purchased earlier from Kuriiri.

CHAPTER 18
BEES

"You can do this." Reya soothes herself. Never before has she wanted to do something so badly the right way. She wanted her seeds to flourish, but she acknowledged that she was a novice. She held the rich potting soil in her hands and inhaled deeply. Urging her to continue, the fragrance of pine bark pushed to the surface. She immediately thought of the forest. A bountiful fragrance with divine energy inhabited the mixture. She chose to sit and run her hands through it. Almost massaging it, Reya was introducing herself to the soil. It felt electric in her body, the raw connection between the earth and her fingers. A few lights on the tips of her fingers began to flicker as she lifted her hands and dove back in. She continued until it just felt right to stop, as if the soil told her it was ready to hold the dear seeds for her. She reached for a small plastic starter container and filled it with the moist soil. She had watched a video where the gardener said it was best to moisten the soil before placing the seeds in the container.

Reya gently opened the unmarked envelope of seeds and placed individual ones in each little hole she made with a pencil. She spoke to them as she placed them in the soil.

"This is the divine soil to start your life. You will be held here by Earth's grace and flourish."

She repeated her words for each seed, like a prayer, it became second nature to her to speak these words.

Five little pots, crowned with plastic wrap, sat above the sink on the kitchen windowsill. Reya sat and stared at them, as if something would erupt from the soil instantly. Invigorated, she watched and listened for a long time, until Valo nudged her for a walk.

"I know it's silly, Valo, but I wanted to watch them for a while. Come on, boy, let's go."

Reya grabs a bottle of water and heads toward the front door. As usual, she glances at the mirror. This time, the light radiating from her head is green, a beautiful, bountiful green that shimmers with lavender highlights. She smiles a little, looks again, and places her hand on her heart.

Valo runs in the meadow like he is crazy. He is especially happy today and the sight brings Reya joy. She glances up toward the mountains and says, "Tomorrow. I will come to meet you tomorrow."

Today, however, she decides to hang out in the meadow and think about her garden to be. She wants to plant some fruits and vegetables and some herbs, too. She begins mapping out in her head the design and how she will do it. Raised beds she decides will be easier. Strawberries she will plant on the pergola in the back so the fruit can create a cover for the porch while keeping the berries off the ground. She decides to plant the herbs around the border of her home. Mainly because herbs can deter bugs but also, she wants the scents to drift in through the cracks of the windows and doors. The smells in the morning will entice her to wake up. She decides on lavender, thyme, mint, oregano, cilantro, and basil.

An interesting fact she discovered is that if citronella grass is planted in pots, the grass, like the candles, will help repel all kinds of insects. Reya amuses herself about the new tidbits of information she is learning. She imagines how her life is changing and all the possibilities the changes will bring.

Valo content, Reya decides to walk with him back home and lounge outside in her backyard. There is a slow breeze today. She relaxes into her chaise lounge and grabs her tablet to research more gardening tips. As she sits, a bee begins hovering over her left foot. She pulls away slowly because she is allergic. She doesn't want to hurt the bee, but she also knows that if the bee stings her it will die, too. Deep breaths. She hopes that if she remains very still, it will fly away. The bee lands on her foot. His delicate legs tickle her skin. She doesn't want to move an inch, but the soft back and forth of the bee's feet make Reya want to scratch the spot it sits on.

Reya knows nothing about bees except for the obvious: honey. The vulnerable little creature sits there for a while as Reya begins to relax and admire his amazingly vibrant colors. Its wings remind her of the stained glass of European churches that come to life when the sunlight hits the glass just right. Timeless, she thought to herself. The bee's wings were timeless. Every flutter of his wings vibrates messages that are passed through the Unknown.

Suddenly, a wave of emotion comes over her, making Reya feel very protective. She wants him to be safe and happy and live a full life doing bee things. As her heart filled up with a surprising unconditional love for the bee, her hands began to move. Her right hand made clockwise motions over the bee gently, so it didn't disturb it. When she did this, she saw the bee in her mind's eye. He had connected to her with a delicate string that looked like fine silk from a spider web, but it wasn't. It was just one single string from her shoulder to the bee's body. He tilted his wings and began to lift off her shoulder. She could feel her body lift with it. She felt like she was floating off the chaise lounge. She wasn't of course, but the sensation left her in wonderment. Like being in a hot air balloon, she imagined. The sight came and went along with the bee. Reya knew at that Moment she would find out more about keeping safe the bees on her property and in the meadow.

Reya opens her tablet and types in "How-to for bees."

CHAPTER 19
FIRST HIVE

Valo is pacing in front of the door. Awakened by his stirring, Reya gets out of bed.

"Do you need to go out?" Reya opens the door to let him go. Still in her pajamas, she stands at the door to wait for Valo to finish his morning routine, but he sits down to watch the mountains instead.

"Ok, boy, we'll go for a walk later, but you got to come in now so I can shower and dress."

Valo just sits and stares at the mountains.

"Valo come here!"

He remains still.

Reya grabs her slippers and walks out to find out what is wrong. Perhaps he has something stuck in his paw and doesn't want to move. She approaches him, puzzled about his behavior.

Valo utters a low, guttural growl; a growl she has never heard before.

"What is it, boy?"

Valo remains a statue, unable to move any muscles except the ones allowing him to make that intimidating growl. Reya looks around the property and toward the forest but doesn't see anything out of the ordinary.

Suddenly, Valo stands up and howls like a wolf for at least thirty seconds before he turns and walks slowly into the house.

Spooked by his behavior, Reya decides to stay home and look up what she will need to order for the new beehive.

"Here's one: https://backyardhive.com/blogs/is-beekeeping-for-me/beekeeping-101-how-to-start-a-beehive."

She starts a list on a post-it.

- Buy:
- Hive
- Protective Suit
- Bee Helmet
- Gloves
- Veil
- Bees

Reya chuckles at the realization she must buy bees. "I guess I thought they just came and set up shop in the beehive once you put it out there. It's like a bee hotel, right?" Reya's comments go unacknowledged by Valo.

After reading several blogs and websites about beekeeping, Reya decides to call Mehlin, a beekeeper who lives in her area. She met him at the farmers market, selling honey. One attractive option presented on some of the blogs was allowing a beekeeper to place hives on her property. She decides she might like that initially. Mehlin, if willing, could help her learn more about the bees and help his hives flourish at the same time. The experience with the little bee guy on the patio touched her so she wanted to help them as much as she could. She left Mehlin a voicemail and asked if they could talk about hives.

She did decide not to wait to order a pollinator from a company called www.honeyflow.com.

It's like a motel for solitary bees. Solitary bees don't colonize like honeybees, but they are important because they pollinate. Bees in general are dying off, a problem she came across during her research. Hives are collapsing and solitary bees are also affected by a deadly disease. Mortified by this discovery, Reya wanted to do her part to help but felt like a rookie needing more knowledge. Reya liked the idea of giving refuge to a single bee with nowhere to go for the night. The thought touched her, and the company that made the pollinator hotels touched her, too. How thoughtful and powerful is this company's mission: To be stewards of these vulnerable little creatures. The company also made beautiful honeybee hives with warm cedarwood. She knew that when it came time to purchase her own, she would buy it from them, too. Warm tears welled up in her eyes. The bees and the little hotels tugged at her emotions. She tried to swallow the tears but decided instead to let them flow. She wiped her face and closed her laptop.

"Ok, Valo, I am off to shower, and then we can walk."

Valo raises his head, tilts it slightly, and then follows her to the shower.

Reya reaches for a raspberry peach blossom and sage soap. The vibrant raspberry scent opens her airways and makes room for the seductive peach fragrance. She feels love in the soap as warmth rises in her. Then it hits her. A deep grounding of sage and a hint of earth, she is lulled into a waking trance. Closing her eyes and slipping into another space, she watches a bird flying over an open shower with a man in it. His nudity shocks her back into reality. She falls forward a bit. Seeing his body aroused her. She places her hand on her heart as if that might stop it from skipping.

CHAPTER 20

FUNERALS

Reya looks at the five pots in the windowsill, astonished that ten days have passed, and nothing is sprouting! Her sigh is heavy and long. The excitement she felt a few days ago has turned into hurt feelings. "I've killed the special seeds," she says to herself. She gathers each one of the pots and takes them to the meadow. She is saddened that nothing came of these seeds. The seeds that lit up her essence and her heart didn't produce even a single leaf. She takes a second to explain to the meadow that she did her best. She thought she was taking care of them correctly.

When her spade hits the earth, the symbols on her arms light up. She lowers her hand into the soil to scoop out space to bury the contents of five pots.

"I'm sorry," she whispers as she buries each in its own little grave. She places one single gentle chicory bloom on each site. Normally, she would consider this a bit dramatic, but she knows the seeds are important and she has failed. Hummingbirds hover, watching her while butterflies take refuge on a few of the chicory blooms. She returns to her house and tells Valo they are taking a ride. She's going back to see Kuriiri.

As she is driving to the fruit stand, tears continue to flow as she remembers the night that she spent in the woods with Aiti, the mother tree. Aiti had told Reya that she was a special being; her presence was vibrating throughout time.

While dreaming under the expanse of Aiti's limbs, Reya heard, *"You've been noticed by others; even the mountains are watching you. They rarely can be bothered with any others besides themselves,"* she says.

Aiti goes on to tell Reya that her being here in this space is not just for her. "The love and tenderness you feel for this land will be shared for many years to come."

Reya doesn't understand her meaning but listens attentively.

"You are the keeper of the seeds, Reya. You will love, hold, and deliver them to the world. This inconspicuous act will touch thousands of lives."

Reya responds, feeling a weight of her significance on her heart and shoulders. "What seeds, Aiti? I don't know what you are talking about nor do I understand what you mean by seeds."

"Don't worry, child." Aiti comforted her with her limbs and embraced her with her foliage. Aiti enveloped Reya with her motherly warmth and Reya, like a small child, fell into Aiti's space. A space of effortlessness, a space of courage and strength, and fearlessness.

The strength Reya felt allowed her to surrender into it. She dropped deeper into her dreams. Waking the next day, she barely remembered the night before but felt amazing and fresh.

As Reya drives, she repeats, "I am so sorry, Aiti." She looks at herself in the rearview mirror and Valo returns her gaze. His eyes, bright and alive, look at her with more love than one heart can hold. Held there in a Moment of grace floating between her space and his, she again feels the link between them like an endless ball of yarn; their connection never severed.

Reya, wanting to lengthen this sweet Moment with Valo, reaches back and strokes his chest briefly before opening the door to get out.

Kuriiri smiles when he sees her and waves gently, welcoming her back.

"How are you today, Reya?"

"Well, I came by because the seeds I bought didn't sprout, and I don't understand why." Her eyes were a little moist. He could see that this meant a lot to her.

"Sometimes you just get a dud seed. Here take these. It's on me," Kuriiri says, passing a handful of the unmarked envelopes to her.

"Oh, Kuriiri, I couldn't. I'm sure it is something I did." Reya assures him.

"No, really. It's fine. I can tell you are fond of the seeds, so just take them." He comforts her with a small pat on her shoulder.

"Ok, but I am paying for those berries and fresh kale over there."

"All right, all right," Kuriiri laughed. "Grab what you need, and I'll ring you up."

Reya drives home with more seeds and starts the entire process over. She's so new to this that she is awkward about screwing it up. She intuitively understands that the seeds must be handled with love and consideration, and she is determined to do this.

The five pots are lined up again, but just like the first time, the seeds do not sprout. Each time she returns to the meadow and says a prayer and then an apology. And each time the meadow responds with butterflies encircling her or sometimes hummingbirds would zip by her head to cheer her up. A bee occasionally attends the ceremony and sits on her sleeve. She would tell herself it was the same bee from the patio, but really, she wasn't sure. She looks out at the field and takes inventory of the mounds and mounds of tiny seed graves, grabs her chest, and sobs into the earth. Her tears flow down her face and into the soil like messengers. The tears morph into veins of light that connect the fallen seeds underground. They are alive. They are willing and they are waiting. Reya stands up and calls Valo to return to the house with her. A cool breeze touches her from the inside out, leaving her with a sense she is being watched. As she opens the back door, she stops and looks over her shoulder. Feeling everything but seeing nothing, she continues inside.

Reya visits Kuriiri several times during the spring and summer season. Each time he consoled her and encouraged her to keep trying. He never charged her for another package of seeds. He always just offered her some words of wisdom. Like:

"Watch out not to water them too much," or "Be sure they get a lot of sun."

Reya's favorite was "Be patient! These things don't always reveal themselves to you right away."

The funny thing was that after about the tenth funeral, she had gone to the local nursery to purchase starter vegetables then put them in raised beds and planters in her backyard. Her vegetable garden was thriving. She was sharing her swiss chard and kale with neighbors and the tomatoes were so abundant she began making a homemade sauce to store for the winter. Her herbs thrived, too. The plants were talking to her differently. She could feel their space like she did that night when she fell into Aiti.

The time she spent in her garden rewarded her with a new intimacy with herself and the symbols. She felt them buzz when she would pick fresh fruit and enjoy it, or when she would reach out and touch the lettuce leaves. She knew that the plants could feel her presence in the garden, and they responded with abundance. They taught her that, with kindness, comes the love of the universe through you so that you are never truly alone. The plants were courting her like lovers, and she fell under each of their spells. Reya's hands moved without notice or awareness. Often, she would find herself in front of a flower or herb and her hands would begin making a clapping sound and then crisscross her body. She would do this several times like in a trance before returning to what she was doing. Afterward, she always felt energized and awake. It was like the experience was thrilling her, but also like it was happening despite her.

Why? and What? were the questions it left her. "Why are my hands moving? What does this all mean? What does it have to do with me? Why am I not getting it?"

Earlier in the spring, she would spend hours trying to answer these questions with no real headway. By summer, Reya had surrendered to the fact that she might never know. She chose, instead, to create a notebook of the hand gestures and markings as best she could. For what use was unclear to her, but it made her feel purposeful and part of something even if she didn't understand it. She also purchased a fire-safe/waterproof box to store the seeds.

Shortly after that, she decided to go see Kuriiri for a visit. She had not seen him in a while since her garden took off. She found herself missing his warm smile and wanted to share with him how successful her garden was, regardless of her failure with the seeds. Reya slowed down, shocked that the stand was gone. There was no sign of Kuriiri. Perhaps he is sick, she thought to herself. I'll try back another day, she comforts herself.

Fall was coming so she knew that she would not attempt to plant the seeds any more this season. Even though she didn't know what was in each envelope, theoretically one might have been a plant that could survive the cold, but she didn't want to risk it. So, she tenderly gathered the mysterious envelopes that held the precious seeds and put them inside a waterproof plastic bag. She placed them in the metal box for next season.

Reya never saw Kuriiri again. She drove by the location of the stand often, but it was never there. She asked about him around town, but no one knew anything. Guilt tugged at her, making her wish she had gone back to the stand sooner. Kuriiri had been so supportive and kind, and she wanted to show him pictures of her thriving garden. It took a lot of work, and she had become immersed in it. She still wanted to get more seeds and share with him some of her veggies. The last time she tried to visit the stand, Reya pulled into the spot where it used to sit. She knew that they were not best friends or anything. Hell, she barely knew anything about him. It was the feeling that he was there for her that made her feel good.

"I'm so selfish," she told herself. She took Kuriiri's presence for granted. She had grown accustomed to him being there and just thought he would always be.

"Really? You thought he'd always be there?" Reya chided herself.

Reya drove slowly away from the empty spot on the road, wanting to sear the feeling into her soul. She never wanted to take someone's grace in her life for granted again.

She looked out the window, closed her eyes for a second, and said goodbye to Kuriiri.

"Thank you for showing up in my life just when I needed you. I hope everything that follows you afterward is filled with enormous joy."

CHAPTER 21

REYA AND MEHLIN

G ardening had become a full-time job: harvesting plants, turning the compost, cooking and storing the fruits and veggies. One of her favorite things was spending time with Mehlin, learning about the bees. He said that next spring she would be ready to tend the hive by herself. Grateful for her help, allowing his bees to thrive in her meadow, he rewarded her with several jars of honey. The labels on the jars read "Reya's Somewhere Honey." The golden yellow honey matched the gold in her eyes. Delighted, she invited Mehlin inside for an iced blend of coriander, peppermint, and bay leaf tea with pickled cucumber sandwiches made with the cucumbers she grew. Reya found that her sense of knowing about the plants and their flavor combinations was multiplying. She didn't know why nor how the combinations she threw together would work, but when she allowed the combinations to flow, the flavors were always miraculous. She added the combinations to the notebook which held the symbols and hand gestures.

Mehlin and Reya grew closer that growing season. She shared with him things from her garden, and he shared with her all he knew about bees. He was touched that she bought pollinator hotels for the solitary bees. He even taught her how to make her own out of things around the house.

He had lived alone for many years. A veteran of the Gulf War, he had trouble relating to civilian life. He moved to the country to get away from the "noise." He told Reya that the hum of the bees relaxed him.

He was broad-shouldered and had large biceps and hands to match. He stood about 6'3" and weighed probably a strong 175 pounds. Muscular but not overdone; his head shaved, a habit he held onto from the military. His eyes were dark brown, almost black, and his skin olive, with tattoos covering his arms and chest. One particular tattoo was of a sword buried in the trunk of a tree. The tree reminded Reya of Aiti. Mehlin was an Army medic before moving here. He was forward deployed most of his career and saw firsthand what destruction by the hands of man can do. He shared with her his battle with PTSD and told her that the medication the VA put him on helped him for a while, but when he tried to ween himself off it, the side effects were worse than the PTSD. One day when he felt especially low, zoned out on the couch, he saw a documentary about bees.

"The whole show just captivated me. I got off the couch and began researching bees and beekeeping and never looked back. I found that the surge of excitement I felt about the bees soothed the anger and frustration I felt about the war."

Reya and Mehlin developed a routine. Every week to ten days Mehlin would come and check on the hives. Afterward, Reya would make them lunch or sometimes dinner.

He was patient with her and taught her about the characteristics of the bees and how to listen for changes in their hums and behaviors. She wanted to tend to them daily, but Mehlin explained to her that she had to resist that urge to smother them with love and allow them space to thrive without interference.

Mehlin would say "You have to let them be bees and just enjoy them as an observer."

Reya would pummel him with questions. "How do you know they are okay? How do you know they are eating enough? How do you know when the honey is ready? How can you tell if they are sick or healthy?"

Mehlin liked that she asked several questions in a row without waiting for an answer to any. He found it endearing. Her enthusiasm reinforced his love of beekeeping. During this time with Reya, he decided to teach others about hives. She was the catalyst for him starting an organization to protect local bees and support the health and wellbeing of hives. Before Reya, he just did it for his own sanity and survival, but now, with her innocence and joy infusing his life, he felt moved to reach out and teach others.

Reya grew closer to him. His passion was infectious. Learning about the pollinators aligned with her desire to grow her own food and develop a stronger relationship with her plants. In the back of her mind, she felt he, too, might be linked to the seeds and her farming here. Who knew, she thought, before meeting him, that bees played such a vital role in growing fruits and veggies.

Her first interaction with that one little bee opened up an entire life for her.

In these Moments when she felt grateful for their friendship, for her a grace in disguise, she would remember Kuriiri and how she never wanted to let her life's focus blind her from everyday miracles of connection.

Their lunches and dinners became a catalyst, too. She looked forward to the mystery of the day's menu. Whenever Mehlin was coming over, Reya would walk to the garden and ask the plants "Who wants to feed Mehlin today?"

Her body would begin by turning around three times and then moving her toward the vegetable or herb that she should cook. The combinations enticed her. After a while, she would just feel the right combinations and see them sometimes inside her mind's eye coming together.

"Today I have roasted chicken. Who else is joining the table today?" Reya asks.

"Kumquats, with sugar beets and thyme salad and a red and purple potato pie," her voice from within speaks.

Mehlin's heart was being healed one bite of food at a time. Every taste washed away some of the pain and suffering he had held on to. After months of him teaching Reya and her feeding him, Mehlin began to look different. His dark, almost black, eyes had changed to a soft oak brown. The tension he held in his jaw relaxed, and his shoulders, although still mammoth and strong, no longer felt guarded to her. The more she fed him, the more he melted, until she was finally able to feel what lay beneath all the pain, suffering, and anger. A heart of gold, she found. A heart that had jagged edges and thorns intertwined with sweet sticky honey. He was beautiful she felt, and the sight of him caught her off guard. She was falling for Mehlin and Mehlin for her.

Neither one of them spoke of their feelings. It was if speaking them out loud might pierce the cocoon that they created for each other. They just weren't ready to blossom yet.

CHAPTER 22
LIFE IS THE ANSWER

Since moving here, Reya has learned so many things but still has many questions with no answers. She still doesn't understand the symbols that lay beneath her skin. She is unsure of their connection to the land and her garden. She doesn't know why the seeds are so important for her to have when they never grow. For some reason, today she wants clarity and longs for the answers that never come. She is hoping for a book or some written doctrine that would spell out the signs' meanings or why she feels what she feels. She wants confirmation from some outside source to assure her that she is not imagining these things.

Today and the days following, Reya must practice patience and living in the current space. She is letting go of the questions; at least she is trying to. She stops looking for verification and decides to just enjoy her life and her difference. Valo, Mehlin, and her space here are the most important things to her now. She wants to cultivate these tangible things that she can relate to.

Reya gazes out her bedroom window, watching the mountains, regretting that she still hasn't made the trek to see them up close. A necessity before, now an item added to her "to-do" list. She lingers in bed, ruminating about the life she has created for herself, astonished and grateful that she has accomplished what she set out to do when she moved here, and more. She never imagined opening her heart to anyone but Valo. As if sensing her unyielding love, he jumps in her bed and showers her with kisses. She nudges him like always and leans into him. His hot breath quickens, sensing her desire to play. She wrestles him down into the blankets with her and pushes her face toward his muzzle so she can kiss him. When she gets close enough to touch his nose, she pops her head under the blanket and hides. He takes his huge paws and digs at the blankets until she comes out. This goes on forever. The thrashing continues, and Valo playfully growls and Reya growls back until they get all worked up and fall into the bed, exhausted. These sweet, tender Moments with Valo are her treasures. She holds them in her heart like valuable belongings one might lock in a safe. She also understands that she is making room for another inside her heart: Mehlin. She is grateful Mehlin understands the remarkable bond she holds with Valo. If not, their friendship would be impossible. Valo will always be at the forefront of her life, and Mehlin supports that. He loves Valo, too.

"Well, Valo, I've goofed off enough. I need to take a shower and get moving."

She heads toward the shower and glances at herself in the mirror. Her eyes look like they are a different color, so she pauses and leans into the countertop to get a closer look. They look like the gold that surrounds her iris is widening. Her eyes haven't changed color, they just look different with an increased ratio of gold. "What the f . . ."

Reya decides to ignore them for now and reaches for a new

bar of soap. She wants "something to ignite my fire" and chooses the soap sitting off to the right of the stack. She turns the knob to the hottest setting so the shower can warm up. Waiting for the steam, she pushes the soap toward her nose. One slow, methodical inhale and she is transported into the bar. Welcoming fragrances of juniper berries and plum waft through her nostrils. She feels a rush of the forest and the force of her hands erupt with light, a bright white light that scares her. She jumps back and drops the soap. The light is gone. Her senses heightened, she takes a minute to gather herself before stepping into the shower.

"You don't have to know why Reya, just go with it," she tells herself. As the shower flows over her, her hands begin moving. Her palms fill with water, rise upward, come together and then separate and lift like a sun salutation, but they outline her head instead and then come back down. This happens several times, and then her right hand makes counterclockwise circles in the palm of her left hand.

Later, outside her master bedroom, Reya sits and writes in the notebook she's crafting. She thinks she might turn it into a book. She'll call it *The Mystery, the Seeds, and a Deep Awakening*. She chuckles. She's been trying to capture the essence of the nature of the plants, and how they relate to the symbols and the glimpses she's experienced since she arrived. She would like to draw a direct correlation from the symbols and seeds to her enhanced intuition. She knows for certain that since they began, she has felt more alive, connected, and focused, but she can't say which symbols or what activation caused the current activity. She decides to just record the byproducts of her time here. Instead of defining the movements or the symbols, she will share with them her observations. She will record the different combinations of plants that make the best soaps, tinctures, and balms. She also decides to describe some of the personality traits she thinks she has noticed in the plants. Reya believes there is so much more to nature than we are able to comprehend and wants to somehow get the message through without sounding like a mental patient.

Reya's Notes

LAVENDER: When I stand next to the plant, I get a funny feeling in my stomach. It has an aura about it that ignites old traditions. It feels like an old friend you invite inside, but they would rather sit outside and talk.

ROSEMARY: It contains an upward motion. It elevates the mind and clears out the cobwebs. It satisfies the mind's desires yet revels in our heart's desires. Keep it near your door to protect your happiness. Keep it near your heart to wear out the depression within.

BELLY BALM: Take the flowers of the rhododendron and mix in passionfruit and beeswax to make a salve to rub on your belly. The luxurious rub calls to your stomach and makes you feel warm inside and loved.

STARLIGHT PLANT (FICUS): In its presence, I feel inspired and dewy. I feel love and laughter. I feel connected to Earth and when I'm near it, I continue to hear the same questions: "Who are you?"

HIBISCUS: Downward movement. The motion of the dew in the morning seeping back into the earth. It feels alive with happiness and joy. It is tender and tenacious. "Be the plenty of your heart," it says.

BEE BALM ELIXIR: Seven drops in a glass of cool water will lift your spirits to the moon. You will awaken from sleep, refreshed, with a sense of knowing within you. Be wakeful. Be alert and willing.

SWEETGRASS: The time of the "Now." The tender leaves are graceful and caring. Sweetgrass is my friend indeed. I love the feel of it in my hands. It fills my cup with profound sadness and then washes it away.

POPULUS: Can wait forever for love. The dying spirit of this plant is rebirthed with fire. It is the dying of this plant that captures its essence. Be kind to them, they are among us always. **CORIANDER:** Plays with fire. It is a plant without boundaries. It beholds no one and can live forever within you. The coriander is a dynamic being. You can feel it blossom in the middle of the day. It will enliven your spirit and give you wings. It believes in you when you cannot. Sprinkle it on your food often.

Feeling due for a break, Reya closes her notebook, stands up, and stretches. She feels drawn to the garden. Talking about the plants makes her want to be near them. She places her feet inside her flip flops and walks outside. Her garden feels her presence arrive. She feels them waiting for her, like friends meeting at a café. Reya senses that they are aware of her. She stands in front of the holy basil plant and saturates its leaves with mist. She is looking at the little purple flowers on it and begins to sing to it.

> *The time is now little flower.*
> *Open and see your life.*
> *Open and feel your life.*
> *Open and begin your life.*
> *You are loved here.*
> *Your love will give life to us all.*

She is humming and singing and her body sways from side to side as she spritzes other plants. In these Moments she feels alive and free, tuned into something beyond her own body and mind. She feels connected to life, growing, blossoming, and ever-changing. She is learning life's lessons through the eyes of her plants. She cries tears of wonder during these Moments. The emotions are too much to express otherwise. She is amazed that she gets to have these experiences. Reya's arms light up like Christmas trees when she feels this way.

Captivated by the Moment and lost in the space, she hears a childlike voice say, "Run!!! Get out!! Hurry!!!" Abruptly disconnected from the Moment, Reya looks for the source.

She calls out, "Is anybody there?"

Valo runs to the front of the house, looking toward the mountains again and begins to growl. It's the same as last time. Reya looks around and sees no one. She looks out her front door to see if someone is there and sees Mehlin pulling in the drive. He notices the disturbed look on her face. Reya had forgotten that he was coming for lunch! She got so distracted with the notebook that lunch completely slipped her mind.

Mehlin approaches and asks her, "What's wrong?"

Reya tells him about the previous Moments and how it shook her. She couldn't explain it, but it felt personal. Mehlin consoled her a bit. "Sit down, Reya, and let me get you a cool drink." Mehlin ushers her to the chaise lounge outside to relax. Valo runs to her side, sitting at attention next to her.

Mehlin tells him, "That's good, Valo, protect her while I go inside."

Mehlin grabs a bottle marked "Wildflower Bourbon" from the shelf. He figures this is the right time for a drink. He fills a shot worth in a square glass and adds a dandelion sugar ice cube. Swirling the cube around, he cools the drink for Reya.

"Here, sip this and tell me exactly what happened."

Reya tells Mehlin about the voice, then Valo, and how it is the second time Valo has behaved that way.

"It is so uncharacteristic of him to growl that way," she tells Mehlin.

"If you are up for it, let's go spend time with the bees. The focus will help you forget this until you have time to process it," he encourages.

"I'm sorry. I forgot about lunch," Reya responds.

"It's fine. We can make it together when we get back from checking the hives. Deal?"

His presence calms her and eases her anxiety. She smiles and tips the glass empty.

"I'd like that," she responds and stands up to hug him. Instead, their faces meet head-on and Mehlin leans in and kisses her tenderly on the lips. Fire and honey flow through her veins. She tastes honeycomb and mint on his lips.

"Nice lip balm," she says, feeling self-conscious. Mehlin's strong hand strokes her hair and neck. He pulls her in closer and she slips deeper into his magical touch. She feels at home, she thinks. Time trickles along while the two hold an embrace for the ages. Mehlin's walls crumble with her tongue's tenderness. She smells of pine trees and ruby red roses.

"The hives will wait." He says as he gently guides her back to the bedroom. Reya and Mehlin spend the next few hours exploring each other. Both lessen their grip on emotional walls and fortresses built up over time, allowing each other to pass their guards with vulnerability and trust. Shades of blue and yellow light encircle Reya as she surrenders to him. She feels the room turning like a wheel. The shift in perspective scares her a little so she holds on to Mehlin even tighter than before. He responds with extra tenderness; grateful she feels safe with him. When the boundaries of reality begin to blur for them both, they explode and call out to each other in ecstasy.

After a long pause, they both look at each other as if for the first time. "I love you, Reya," Mehlin says as he caresses her face.

"I love you, too," Reya smiles as wide as her mouth will allow.

Mehlin gets a silly look in his eyes and says, "How about that lunch you were going to make me?"

"I'm starving, too," she says, grabbing for a robe as she jumps out of bed.

Filled with new emotions and feelings, her heart is buzzing. She feels alive on another level.

She looks in the refrigerator and says, "Who wants to play in my kitchen with me?" Reya enters into a frenzied trance, unleashing all her feelings and creativity in her kitchen. Before she realizes it, the countertops are covered with enough food to feed the town.

Smoked grass-fed cheddar cheese with pickled onions baked on flatbread with garlic-infused olive oil, thyme, and oregano.

Grilled beef tenderloins sautéed in butter with chilled asparagus soup.

Spicy green papaya and carrot salad tossed with rice wine vinegar and cilantro.

Custard tartlets with pomegranate and cognac reduction drizzled on top. Fresh whipped cream.

Mehlin looks at the table and can't believe his eyes, "You did all of this for lunch?"

Reya says with a smile. "Look at the clock! We missed lunch; it's dinner time."

They both fill their plates and devour the feast. Mehlin feeds Reya whipped cream with his fingers and wraps her in his arms. Both of them curl up on the couch. Valo sits nearby, watching and waiting for an opportunity to jump on the couch with them. Sensing him feeling left out, Reya strokes Valo's back.

Mehlin calls to him, "Get up here, too." Valo jumps in between them and scoots them apart, as if reclaiming Reya for himself.

With full stomachs and hearts, Reya and Mehlin fall asleep together in her bed for the first time. She backs into him, so he fills in the curves of her body. He watches her drift in and out of sleep until he, too, gives in to his exhaustion.

Mehlin wakes early to complete the remaining work on his hives that he didn't do the day before. He jots a quick note and places it under a candle he sees nearby. He doesn't want to turn on lights and risk waking her from what appears to be an amazing slumber.

Didn't want to wake you. Off to the Hives.

Call you later.
XOXO

CHAPTER 23
GLIMPSE INTO THE UNKNOWN

*Renaissance blue background with paintbrush strokes of baby yellow
and soft white
Infinite adorned ornate mirrors hang from invisible strings
Some rotating clockwise while others counterclockwise
Faces, places appear and disappear randomly in the mirrors
Mirrors opposite each other catch the reflection in the other, passing on
to the next
Infinite mirrors, infinite rotations, infinite possibilities for life*

CHAPTER 24
THE MOUNTAINS SIT UP

Reya wakens to the smell of pine and citrus from the candle Mehlin left burning. She gets out of bed and sniffs the aroma while looking at the note.

"Valo, looks like it's just you and me today." Feeling refreshed and full of energy, she looks out the window.

"How about we hike to the mountains?" Cocking his head to the left and right, watching her every word, Valo jumps on hind legs and hugs Reya. "I guess that is a yes! Ok, I am going to shower, get dressed, and pack so we can go."

Reya grabs for the peony and patchouli body scrub along with a daisy shower gel and washes away Mehlin's scent. She decides not to wash her hair. She'll shower again when she and Valo return. Reya goes over the invisible checklist in her head. Since she hasn't ever made it to the mountains, she is unsure how long the hike will take. She is guessing it's about thirteen miles roundtrip. She considers she may not make it back tonight so grabs a bedroll and a weatherproof blanket, just in case, extra food and water for sure, along with a flashlight. The checklist is revised out loud as she simultaneously walks the situation through her mind.

As a tradition, Reya stops at the door and looks in the mirror. She swears the image in the mirror is smiling back at her today. She feels giddy about Mehlin and thinks perhaps that is what she sees. Before she closes the door, she looks around to make sure everything is turned off. She fires off a text to Mehlin, so he knows where she is.

Hiking to the mountains today with Valo.

May spend the night if I can't get back before dark.

XOXO
Reya

Lost in her thoughts, she replays last night over and over. Valo runs ahead, as always leading the way. She is excited because before reaching the mountains, she will pass by Veli and the Mother tree. She hasn't seen either since Aiti told her about the seeds. She felt anxious about telling her that she failed but decided to keep moving forward. The meadow looked especially beautiful today. The flashes of her first hike and introduction to the land fill her with nostalgia. She loves her home and feels so much appreciation for the land beneath her.

As Reya steps on the Earth, the seeds below feel her presence. Her arms twitch a little, but she pushes forward. She doesn't want to get distracted in the meadow.

"The mountains await," she tells herself. Reya passes Veli and her arms make an "X" motion. She nods her head and tells him she cannot stay to play today. She is going to see the mountains. The Aspens' leaves move together, sending a small current of energy toward Reya. She feels it land slightly on the nape of her neck.

She chuckles a little and still tells herself, "Nope, you can't play with them either."

The last time she approached Aiti, Reya was greeted by

butterflies and hummingbirds but not today. The forest is unusually quiet. She doesn't really mind the quiet but does find it odd. Even more odd is the space in the earth that once fed and held Aiti. Reya looks around, wondering if she missed a turn or veered off the path somewhere, but intuitively she feels she is in the right place.

For the brief Moment she thought she may be losing it, she saw the six rocks that surround Aiti remained. Her court, the six other trees were also gone. "What the hell?" Reya says, disconcerted. She looks at Valo as if he should know what is happening, but he just circles and smells the dirt where Aiti used to be.

Feeling a little lightheaded she decides this is a good time to take a break. She pulls some jerky out of her pack and hands it to Valo. For herself, she selects oatcake with cranberries, dates, and almonds. Half of the oatcake is dipped in white chocolate with coconut sprinkled on top. She grabs her water bottle and drifts. It doesn't make sense. They have had great weather this season. No huge storms could have taken out the trees. There are no truck marks or huge holes that might indicate someone took the trees. She is mystified.

Realizing she may never see Aiti again, she feels guilty for waiting so long to visit. She felt ashamed about the seeds and being caught up in her own beautiful life with her garden and Mehlin. She simply thought the trees would always be there, like the rest of the forest. She told herself she needed to build up her courage to face Aiti, but she had obviously taken too long.

Acknowledging there is nothing she can do right now, Reya pushes forward to finally see the mountains. After hiking about 45 minutes more, she sees the base of the mountains ahead. She takes her backpack off her shoulders and tells Valo to post next to her. Hands up, palms out, she makes small circles in front of her face. She makes several rotations and then lowers them in front of her as if catching water from a faucet.

She closes her eyes and says, "I am Reya," and then she waits. She doesn't hear or feel anything. The mountains do not call back to her. She looks down at Valo and decides to just sit on the ground below them and wait a while. She can feel them, sensing their enormity and timelessness. She decides perhaps she's too small for them to bother with. They are after all, endless.

Reya leans back against Valo and decides to take it easy. If it feels right to stay the night, she will. She has about an hour before she must decide. After that, she'll have to stay because it will be too dark to hike back.

Back at Reya's home the bed still shows evidence of the night before along with the dirty dishes piled in the sink. Both Reya and Mehlin, too distracted to worry about washing them, left the remnants of dinner without a second thought.

The candle that Mehlin lit for Reya is still burning. As the very last bit of wick burns off, bubbles noisily, and then pops, a small ember wafts off the tip of the wick and floats into the air. One little golden ember lands on a single blade of wild grass near the border of Reya's backyard. Seconds pass and a little red and blue flame erupts.

The meadow is on fire. The flames engulf the space quickly. This time of day, the bees are gathering pollen and nectar, so the hives are empty except for the queen and her caregivers. The small grasshoppers, snakes, rabbits, foxes begin to run in the direction of the mountains, fleeing to get out of the path of the fire. The heat so intense, Reya's house and garden catch fire. Sparks send more embers into the surrounding field and the intensity grows. The beautiful soaps by the shower begin to lose shape as they melt from the heat. The bedroom where Reya and Mehlin made love the night before is engulfed in smoke, suffocating any evidence of love or tenderness that lingered. Reya's drying herbs and essential oils made the fires smell seductive. The tragedy smelled glorious and sacred. Smoke was seen for miles, someone from town passing by calls the all-volunteer fire department to report the fire. Mehlin, a member of the team gets a call. He hangs up the phone and races toward Reya's house. "Please don't let her be there, God. Please!" he prays.

Building intensity, the fire dances across the meadow toward the forest. The quaking Aspen witnessing the horror, send ripples through the Unknown to the animals, the trees, and the mountains.

VIIME, LASNA, AND TULEVAISUUS FEEL A TICKLE FROM THE UNKNOWN AND DECIDE TO INVESTIGATE THE DISTURBANCE.

Reya snaps out of her daydream when she hears Valo growl. It is the same growl she witnessed at home when Valo was outside looking toward the mountains. She jumps up to see if someone or something is out there and sees smoke instead. Reya's cell phone doesn't have any bars. She can't call for help. She grabs her pack, water, and the rest of the gear and decides to ascend the lower levels of the mountain to get a better vantage point. "Perhaps someone is clearing out some land," she says to Valo. Valo continues to growl and cannot be contained by Reya's commands. She is afraid. Panicking inside, she grabs on to Valo and tells him to climb.

THE MOUNTAINS, STARTLED BY THE COMMOTION, RAISE THEIR HEADS TO SEE A BURNING FOREST BELOW. VIIME CLIMBS ON LASNA TO GET A BETTER LOOK. ROCKS SHOWER THE GROUND BELOW AS LASNA PUSHES BACK.

Reya, higher up, starts to feel the ground shake a bit and sees rocks from above falling off the ridges of the mountains above. She and Valo run to get out of the way. When she fully stands upon a higher ridge, Reya freezes. Past the tree line now, she sees the forest and the meadow are on fire. She is frozen in shock, watching the flames dance so beautifully across the land. She cannot see her home from this vantage point, but her stomach tells her it is gone.

Hysterical, tears are coming down her face, yet she is unaware she is crying. Animals running and birds sound like they are screaming. Reya doesn't notice she is paralyzed. She cannot outrun the fire. It is too powerful and strong. The air is starting to get heavier with smoke and the heat from the wall of fire coming their way appears insurmountable. She takes a hand towel and a handkerchief out of her backpack and drenches them with water. She ties one around her mouth and nose and does the same for Valo.

TULEVAISUUS STANDS ON BOTH LASNA'S AND VIIME'S BACK. TRYING TO PLAY KING OF THE MOUNTAIN, TULEVAISUUS DOESN'T CARE ABOUT THE FIRE. ROCKS FALL FROM BOTH SIDES OF THE RIDGES AS THE MOUNTAINS PLAY. VIIME PUSHES TULEVAISUUS' LEG OUT FROM UNDER HIM. THE TRIPOD TOPPLES OVER.

Each step she takes away from the fire is met with more rock-fall. Reya fears she'll never see Mehlin again. She grapples with the possibility that she and Valo will not make it out of the fire. Things start slowing down and she tells herself. "It is true; things go in slow motion just before you die." She fumbles for her cell phone and tries to send a text hoping it will get through somehow.

I'm sorry. I love you. Always
Reya

"Valo! Come!" Reya shouts, "We have to try to get higher." She climbs and dodges rocks that periodically pummel her from above. The mountains sound like they are falling around her, but they are opening around her instead. Suddenly, a large, jagged crevasse appears out of nowhere. She looks at it, trying to determine if she and Valo can fit in it, but then what?

TULEVAISUUS GETS BACK UP AND VIIME KNOCKS OUT HIS OTHER LEG. TULEVAISUUS BEGINS LAUGHING AND PUNCHING THE OTHER TWO WITH HIS LEGS. THE GROUND BELOW SHIFTS AND RUMBLES. VIIME SITS UP A LITTLE AND PREPARES TO POUNCE AGAIN.

Reya falls and holds onto the rocks as they move and sway. She wonders how an earthquake happens at the exact time as a fire. The crevasse widens even more. Can she and Valo wait out the fire in there? She ponders. What if a landslide blocks Valo and her in? She feels like the mountains are alive. Her face hot from first degree burns, she is rubbing her eyes; they itch of smoke and dust. The cracks get larger and deeper into the mountains and Reya decides that it is their only chance of survival. She takes one more look back as the fire barrels toward them. She closes her eyes and imagines her home and all the love and gratitude she feels for it then jumps into the Unknown. The crevasse opens further and then closes and then opens again. She feels like she is in a house of mirrors and can't tell which mirror is the real one. Valo and her image dance in the mirrors and rotate around and around. One crack opens, then darkness and the Unknown pulls them deeper and deeper into the mountains. She cannot hear anything anymore. Complete and utter silence. She cannot see Valo, but she feels him nearby. Unsure if she is alive anymore, she stands motionless.

LASNA, DETERMINED TO GET ON TOP OF THE TRIPOD, ROLLS UNDER THE OTHER TWO AND JUMPS. ALL OF THEM LAUGH, REALIZING THEY HAVEN'T FELT THIS AWAKE IN AGES. ROLLING, TOSSING, TURNING THE WRESTLING CONTINUES.

Reya feels her feet shift forward but she does not feel like she is moving them on her own. The symbols on her arm flicker on with a low humming noise surrounding her. The air shifts each time there is an opening and then changes as the walls of the mountain close behind her. She doesn't know where she is nor the direction she is headed, but she knows she cannot go backward.

The heat from the fire beats Mehlin back. Reya's home lost in a storm of smoke, the firemen are too late. They douse the remaining walls and roof with water, but all the volunteers know two things: No one could survive a fire like that, and the home is totaled. The only thing they could do is attempt to put the fire out and ensure there are no lingering hot spots that could flare up again. His fellow firefighters hold Mehlin back as he unleashes the full strength of his PTSD.

"I have to know if she was in there." Screaming, his words are nonsense to everyone but him. He doesn't realize that screams and groans are the only things coming out of him right now. It takes four of them to hold him down. The EMT's arrive and the station captain asks if they can sedate Mehlin. They don't want him running into the fire, placing any other team members in jeopardy if they must go in after him. Valium carries him off to a deep place; a place he hasn't visited in a very long while. The depths of despair; a place he thought no longer available or open to him since meeting Reya. The darkness opens up to him like an old friend. A blanket of sadness wraps around him tightly as he sits on the ground, beaten.

The team loses footing as the ground shakes. Distracted, they look toward the mountains. It sounds like the mountains are falling but they resist the urge to investigate.

Reya puts one step in front of the other. "Forward," she thinks to herself. Periodically she sees little pulses of light flash. The lights never stay long enough to illuminate where she is. Still, endless silence. She feels cold and frightened again. She can't hear the hum nor Valo nor anything. She, like an android, just keeps pushing her feet forward.

Viime, Lasna, and Tulevaisuus watch the fire rip through the landscape until it lands at their feet. They are not amused. Viime bends down and blows it back. The wind he makes sounds like a tornado. The force rips the bark off

THE TREES, NOW BRITTLE WITH THE CHARRED TRUNKS REMAIN-
ING. LASNA LAUGHS AT VIIME AND PUSHES TULEVAISUUS.

It feels like hours pass to Reya. She accepts that she will never see Mehlin, her garden, or the bees again. Her only consolation is that Valo is with her and her notebook is locked tightly away in the fire-safe box she purchased months ago. Silence breaks with a deafening sound of water. Reya thinks she hears a stream as it is barely audible, but the gentle continuous flow is there. She feels the water calling to her. Although she can't feel him, she calls to him anyway. "Valo, come on boy."

Reya runs toward the water and hears Aiti's voice. "Welcome home, Reya and Valo."

EPILOGUE

A fter months of mourning her loss, he did something no one expected. Mehlin purchased the scorched earth that once held Reya's home. He could not imagine anyone else's spirit filling the space the way she did. In his heart, he knew that it was selfish to deny the place to others, but he was too broken and angry to care. Instead, Mehlin left what remained of the house untouched. The burnt remnants were all that were left of her, and he wanted to hold on to them. He did not care if others thought it macabre, he still felt her there. He still felt her tenderness toward the bees and the trees and ultimately toward him. He spent days visiting the property, sitting on the ash covered foundation where he would swear that she was still talking to Valo. Mehlin sometimes secretly wished Valo survived so he might have something left of her. Since their bodies were never found, he was unable to bury them. Instead, he enshrined their memories on the property where they once lived, loved, and played.

As the land recovered, he brought a few hives and placed them in the same spot where the others perished. He knew the bees humming would bring Reya joy. He gave the honey away to friends in the community denying himself any sweetness. Punishing himself, he still felt responsible for the fire. After all, it was the candle that he lit for her that morning which started it. That is at least what he gleaned from the fire inspector's report. Reya's fire was the last fire he ever ran toward. Volunteering for the fire department was no longer something he could or would endure. He missed his friends from the department but not enough to put the uniform back on.

Mehlin's visits to Reya's property continued for many years but diminished with his age. Traveling to her land was no longer safe for him to do alone. He began losing track of time and was often confused about the day of the week or even the year. Friends from his community volunteered to drive him out to sit with her. Everyone who knew him also knew their story and how much he loved her. They whispered behind his back about how broken he was, how a once strong, passionate man who enjoyed life closed his heart entirely to any other love forever. There were times before the end that he forgot entirely about the fire and had to relive the sorrow of losing her all over again. Mehlin never stopped hearing Reya and Valo. He also never let go of the property. Buyers offered him above the valued price all the time, but the answer was always the same. "She's still out there. This is her home."

Continued in book 2: The Greenhouse
https://books2read.com/the-greenhouse

GLOSSARY

Reya: Flowing, The gardener
Valo: Light, Reya's dog
Veli: Brother, Quaking aspen tree
Aiti: Mother-in-house, Mother Tree/Dragon blood tree
Kuriiri: Courier, Farmer who owns the fruit stand.
Terve: Healthy, sound, strong, Farmer and owner of the Greenhouse
Teija: gift of God, Terve's wife,
Kaia: Pure, Terve's daughter
Kali: River, Terve's son
Rohkea: Brave, Terve's horse
Nea: Flower, Terve's mother
Yli: Beyond, one of the giants/mountains
Lasna: Present, one of the giants/mountains
Viime: Past, one of the giants/mountains
Tulevaisuus: Future, one of the giants/mountains
Avaruus: Space, Pilot
Ajatella: Remember, Navigator and Avaruus' friend
Tieto: Knowledge, Co-pilot and Avaruus' friend
Sielu: Soul

Somewhere: Where Reya lives and gains the seeds.

Somewhere Else: Where Terve lives and the Greenhouse is built.

Another Place: Where Anushka lives along with the Apothecary.

Andrena: Species of bee, Apothecary employee

Colletidae: Species of bee, Apothecary employee

Apidae: Species of bee, Apothecary employee

ACKNOWLEDGMENTS

For my publisher Daniel Stombaugh at Lakeview Publishing. Your spirited guidance and positive perspective are everything. You championed me through this entire process, and I always feel supported as an artist. I wish you, the team at Lakeview and your family boundless waves of gratitude and sanctuary for your life ahead. Thank you for believing in me.

To my editor Carol Williams. The delightful sharing that erupted from working with you is priceless to me. Your kindness and tenderness were present throughout the process. As a Master Gardener you were the absolute right person to take this excursion with me.

To Bobby Barnhill, cover illustrator, thanks for your patience and wisdom beyond my recognition of what was possible for this cover. You are a professional and a gift. I am grateful for your light.

To Elizabeth Buck who gave me and Rembrandt a place to create this story when I had nowhere else to go. Thank you for your comfort and your endless giving heart and spirit.

Finally, I must again recognize the mysteries that sit in front of us all waiting patiently for us to wake up. For the tenderness that is available to all of us when we connect and tune in to nature, life and the existence of things beyond our understanding.

ALSO BY SONYA YOUNG

Folding Flags: https://books2read.com/folding-flags

The Gardner: https://books2read.com/the-gardner
The Greenhouse: https://books2read.com/the-greenhouse
The Apothecary: https://books2read.com/the-apothecary

Follow her author journey at: https://books2read.com/ap/8ZjMQj/
Sonya-Young

ABOUT THE AUTHOR

Sonya Young, author of **Folding Flags** is a veteran, artist and a nature enthusiast. After serving 20 plus years of military service and completing her MS from the University of San Diego, she turned her focus toward the artist within. Her inspiration for this book is rooted in her desire to share her experiences with nature and how it unfolds in the most unexpected ways. A resident of Las Vegas, she has spent countless hours hiking where she confesses her heart and mind feel connected totally to life.

Connect with her on Instagram or Facebook. View her visual art via her website www.artbysonyayoung.com

facebook.com/SY2021Author

instagram.com/artbysonyayoung

Want to Publish Your Book?

We Can Help!

* Manuscript Editing

* Book Cover

* Book Formatting

*Illustrations

* Publishing through all major retailers
(Amazon, Kobo, B&N, Apple)

* Paperbacks & eBooks

* Blurb Writing

* Audio Books

* Choose Your Own Package

* Author Retains <u>ALL</u> rights

We're here to help!

"Everyone has a story to tell, only the courageous will find a way to get it told. Let my team and I help you become courageous!"

LAKEVIEW
PUBLICATIONS

www.LakeviewPublishers.com

www.ingramcontent.com/pod-product-compliance
Lightning Source LLC
Chambersburg PA
CBHW030234180626
46810CB00008B/3118